THULE

A WEIRD MENACE NEO-PULP

(REVISED EDITION)

By David Eveleigh

Table of Contents

The darkness was almost complete. Only a slight sliver of lamplight crept through the drawn blinds and into the roach infested motel room. It stretched across dilapidated wooden floorboards to a slowly rotting desk, where it illuminated the Professor's face in a low orange glow. His eyes darted to the window as an air raid siren wailed somewhere in the distance. Hearing it was a reminder of the sword which hung above his head and of the evil force that he was faced against.

He held the telephone's receiver in his sweaty palm. The Professor was convinced that the line was bugged, but he had no choice. He could not risk being seen in the bombed-out London streets. After all, who knew how many members of His Majesty's kingdom were really spies for the German Fatherland?

"Don't worry," he said, "the notebook is still safe. But please hurry. If the Nazis find out I'm here, my life won't be worth spit. If *she* finds out I'm here..."

The Professor stopped in mid-sentence. He listened to the voice on the other end. However, whatever words of assurance it offered him appeared to have the opposite of their desired effect.

"No," he interrupted, "you don't understand. That woman is diabolical. She's a monster!"

He spent a moment in silence. Outside, he heard the rumbling engine of a Mercedes halt just below his window.

"Alright," the Professor said, "twenty minutes. I'll be expecting you."

He hung up the phone and breathed a cool sigh.

It will all be over soon, he told himself. However, both his thoughts and his newly found calmness were interrupted by a brief flicker across the blinds, followed by a sharp noise in the dark.

Schreck...

The sound repeated itself, drawing closer as it did so.

Schreck...
Schreck...

Schreck...
The White Baron, the Professor thought. His face grew pale. The darkness that had once protected him from enemy eyes now hid the most lethal of all assassins.

An assassin that was closing for the kill.

The Professor grabbed the telephone, but it was already too late. He felt a violent pinch on his arm. Then came the dizziness. He stumbled forward into the blackness as it became even deeper. The sliver of light faded from his eyes, until he was swimming in an inky abyss. His knees buckled and he collapsed face down on the floor, where he lay while his body cooled and stiffened.

***

Twenty minutes passed in total stillness. The siren still echoed from over the horizon, its operators unaware that the approaching raid had already claimed its first victim. The Professor's corpse remained untouched by everything except the orange sliver, which shone a spotlight over his gaping mouth and staring eyes. Suddenly, the doorknob rattled. A light tap followed, accompanied by a whisper.

"Professor?"

The knob rattled again, but the lock refused to yield. Then came the loud banging of a body slamming itself against the door. Finally, the wood splintered and gave way. Light poured in from the hall, framing the corpse in a rectangular yellow glow. But that same light also framed a silhouette standing at the threshold. The figure stepped towards the body and knelt beside it. It was the shape of a man whose hair was greying at the temples, his face lined by years of hardship. Around his neck, he wore the collar of a priest. He crossed himself and uttered a short prayer for the Professor. Hopefully, the man's death would not be in vain.

The priest felt the floorboards underneath the desk until he found one that was loose. Removing it, he discovered a small, leather-bound notebook. He smiled as he opened it. This was the key that he was searching for. A weapon in the war for the souls of humanity. He began to read the pages eagerly.

"I have discovered," the Professor had written, "that in his quest to create a master race, Hitler has turned to the occult for aid. An organization calling itself 'The Thule Society' is spearheading his dream, combining science with black magic in utterly inhuman experiments. Overseeing this whole operation is some kind of self-styled 'priestess' calling herself Efeu, whose very name strikes fear in the hearts of both Allied and Axis officers alike. One byproduct of her experiments is creature nicknamed 'The White Baron'. This monster..."

The priest's attention was broken by a sharp noise in the dark.

Schreck...

Schreck...

He realized that he wasn't alone. The Professor's killer was still in the room. The priest backed away from the shadows, seeking the protection of the yellow light, as the sound drew closer.

Schreck...

Schreck...

His eyes darted to the doorway. It had been locked when he'd arrived. The only other way inside would have been the window. Yet it was only open a couple of inches. Nobody could have squeezed through such a small crack.

Nobody human, at any rate, he thought.

Schreck...

The noise was so close that he could almost reach out and touch it. His left hand explored the desk behind him in search of something to defend himself with. His fingers touched cold metal. A letter opener.

Schreck...

The priest swiped his weapon in the direction of the sound, but cut only the empty air.

Schreck...

A shadow brushed past his cheek. He lunged for it with all his might, plunging his blade into the darkness, and felt the weapon make contact.

For an instant, an unholy screech drowned out the sound of the air raid siren. But it died almost as soon as it had begun. The priest pulled the letter opener out of its target and switched on the lights.

Lying on the floor in a pool of black ichor was a large white insect. It reminded him of a grasshopper in some ways. The priest's eyes fell back on the journal.

"One byproduct of her experiments is a creature nicknamed 'The White Baron'. This monster has been bred from the common locust using Efeu's devilish methods. It is larger in size, albino, and has developed a stinger containing a deadly neurotoxin. Furthermore, its brain has progressed to the point where it can be trained to kill on command, making it an almost perfect agent of murder."

The priest closed the book and sighed. A hundred of the Third Reich's demonic secrets were contained within its pages, secrets that he could now expose to the proper authorities. Nervous that he might have been seen, he fled from the motel room, down the stairs and into the war torn streets of London. He tread as stealthily as possible down those roads, sticking close to the alleys in case he would have to make a break for it. Although orange lamplight illuminated his path, the siren acted as a reminder that he would have to find a shelter before the Luftwaffe arrived. However, his ears detected a second sound. The soft thunder of a car engine was dogging his heels. He kept his pace steady and unassuming until a blinding pair of headlights came out of the night. Moving like lighting, they pulled up and halted right beside him. The priest stopped in his tracks and watched as two figures emerged from a freshly polished Mercedes. The first was a tiny man wearing round glasses and sporting a toothbrush moustache, a pale shadow of the Fuhrer whom he was trying to emulate. But the second, she was tall and magnificent beast. She was dressed as though for a funeral, in a long black dress and a matching veil, and wore a perfume that smelled of bitter almonds. She almost seemed to float as she approached. Although he could see nothing of her face beneath that cloth, the priest felt as if an ocean blue eye were staring into his soul. An eye which saw everything that lay in his heart. When the veiled woman spoke, it was in a foreign dialect that he did not recognize. Fortunately, her companion acted as interpreter.

"Efeu is pleased that you have found the Professor's notebook for us." He said. His mistress held out her long, curled fingernails expectantly. But the priest only shrank from her. Shrank from that damned eye which could penetrate his very being. It did more than observe him. It was as if a will infinitely more powerful than his own were impressing itself upon his mind. Even her fragrance multiplied until it threatened to suffocate him.

"I'll never give this to you," he said, "what you are doing is unholy. You people will burn in Hell."

Efeu laughed and uttered something in her own tongue.

"Unholy?" her companion translated. "Father, don't you see that we are your only defence? Oh, our methods may seem harsh. But do you really think that the atheistic Bolsheviks in the Soviet Union will tolerate your presence? Mark my word, in a hundred years, maybe less, they will have successfully demonized you and all your caste in the public eye, just as we too have been demonized. Instead of being praised as God's teachers, you shall be spat on as fanatics and pedophiles. Tell us, where will the souls of the faithful stand then?"

The priest said nothing. What could he say when faced with that eye and its superhuman will? Under its gaze, the scent of almond perfume became a gas chamber. He choked as he struggled to hold his breath. Unfortunately, the need for air proved overpowering. He inhaled deeply and filled his lungs with Zyklon-B. Like opium fumes, it made a dream pass before his eyes. He had a vision of alien hordes gathering in the east. He saw them rising up. They came to strip this land of its race and culture. Of its religion. The only thing standing between them was this supernatural creature who beckoned him with an ivory claw. So, with a tremor in his soul, the priest chose to give up his prize.

"Danke." The veiled woman said after he handed her the notebook. He watched as she and her interpreter climbed back into the Mercedes and sped off into the night. As their taillights disappeared, he found himself wondering why he had ever opposed Hitler in the first place.

"There is no freedom from illusion. There is only the illusion of freedom."
-Translated from Efeu's private journals

The End

CARNAGE CASTLE PART 1

Chapter 1

"Over the years, many have scoured through historical records hoping to learn the Third Reich's occult secrets. Little did they realize that the mysteries they sought lay right in front of their faces. By bearing the ancient rune symbols on our uniforms and banners, we achieved an inner, spiritual transformation, elevating us above the common folk to a level akin to Nietzsche's overman. Understand that the true art of magic is not witchcraft. It is runelore, the use of symbols to control perception, both in oneself and in others. Magic words do not change reality, but change how it is seen and valued. Every battle is fought with runelore. It is a blade that cuts through any enemy defence.

Throughout history, there has only ever been one war; the conflict of ideals that takes place inside the human mind. Everything else, the swords, the shields, the bullets, the bombs, the panzers, the blitzkriegs, have never been anything more than an extension of that. However, the theatre of war is not a battlefield. It is a shopping centre. Those who fight within it are not soldiers, they are merchants. Ideas are their merchandise. Runelore is their marketing strategy.

These scribblings of mine which you are now reading form the blackest of all bibles. They are not words for the weak, who will see only evil and lack the depth to perceive anything beyond it. These words are for the hardened, who do not flinch at horror and find purpose in struggle.

For it takes courage to look in the mirror.

And if you spend time studying your own reflection, you may find that you look a lot like us."

-Translated from Efeu's private journals

The world had grown soft. It was many generations since true tyranny had last reared its head in civilized society. Although numerous souls boasted of their strength and intelligence, none of them proved to be anything but helpless when a new Caesar finally did take the throne.

The conflict that followed this pharaoh's ascension could not rightly be called a war. It was a genocide. It was Rome burning bright enough to light up the heavens. It was Babylon crushed beneath the weight of its own excesses. It was Atlantis sinking into the sea.

One era ended and another commenced.

There was no moral to the story. There was only history.

The fire had begun so dimly that the first sparks remained undetected until it was too late. An observant eye could have possibly seen them in the orange glow of the setting sun. Dusk was creeping over the village of Wewelsburg, weaving it in an aura of mystery. To Katrine, there was magic in the sunset. The sky had become a fireball, as though the gods had set it ablaze to entertain the mortals. Katrine, or "Kitty" as all her friends called her, smiled to herself, amused at having a poet's soul. But she could not help it. She saw magic all around her; in the wind, in the trees, in the lush, green grass and the call of the birds. Even the old castle had its own, albeit darker, brand of magic. She was leaning her back against the jagged walls of the ancient fortress and felt a shiver as she glanced at it from over her shoulder. During the second world war, Wewelsburg Castle had been Hitler's Mecca. It was here that the SS were said to have sought help from the powers that lay beyond the mortal sphere. Its grim history had not begun with the Nazis either. The citadel was originally built in the early sixteen hundreds for the Archbishops of Paderborn, who put it to use as a torture chamber for the Inquisition. Over one hundred thousand accused witches and heretics met gruesome ends within its catacombs before the Fuhrer was even born. Perhaps some strongholds are merely built on a bad foundation.

Today, however, Wewelsburg Castle served a far less ominous duty. While much of it was still closed to the public, the renaissance battlement was refurbished and reopened as a youth hostel. Kitty had spent a night there once after a fight with her father. She recalled being shocked by how modernized so much of it had become. Now, big, big plans had been made to bring Wewelsburg into the twenty-first century and leave all that unpleasant business in the past. A celebrated foreign architect was even brought in to lend her special touch to the building's new design. It was because of that woman that Kitty now found herself waiting by the castle's gate. The architect had a son who was in dire need of companionship in this strange land. As Kitty waited for the boy to arrive, the wind began to pick up and she could swear that she heard the cries of one hundred thousand witches spitting curses at a world that presumed to forget them. With those cries came the soft roar of a motor. On the streets below the castle's perch, she spied a vintage Mercedes. It was jet black, polished to a shoemaker's shine and stuck out from the rest of the village as an oddity out of time. Kitty could not recall anyone in town owning such a vehicle. Its presence unnerved her. She watched it drive past slowly and was possessed by the feeling that someone inside had their eye on the fortress. For a moment, the breeze carried the scent of bitter almonds. The car vanished around a corner and the seemingly haunted wind died down. But the feeling remained. The feeling of a stranger's eye stabbing into her flesh.

The heavens turned blacker by the second, as if they were a river of blood that was being polluted with a venomous ichor. Made anxious by the approaching darkness, Kitty glanced once more towards the gate of the youth hostel. She had been waiting outside for a full twenty minutes and was getting antsy. But, at long last, she now spied her partner in tonight's mischief crossing the courtyard to meet her.

"I'm coming." Casey said softly before she even had a chance to call to him. The boy seemed to have an uncanny knack for always knowing what Kitty was going to say before she said it. Sometimes, she suspected that he could read her mind. She dared not ask him about it upfront. She was far too afraid of sounding silly if her suspicions were wrong and her copper-headed companion never brought the subject up himself. So, it remained an elephant in the room, at least in Kitty's mind. She thought that Casey was rather

handsome. His long hair, as red as Thor's own beard, was tied back in a ponytail and trailed after him like a chestnut dragon. His distant eyes were as green as Alme Valley and seemed haunted by something which he dared not voice. When they were not turned downwards in shyness, they had an uncommon keenness, which was emphasized by long lashes that any girl would be jealous of. She might have considered having him as a summer boyfriend if trying to get near him were not like trying to get behind the Berlin Wall.

Spending time with the boy was not a choice, but a favour to her father. Casey's mother had dragged him halfway across the world so that he could bear witness to her renovations on the castle, which promised to be the pinnacle of her career as an architect. If he had any friends or family in his own country, he never spoke of them. He did mention that he was of German descent on his father's side. But, although he was visiting the land of his ancestors, he could not utter a word of the language. Luckily, Kitty's English was pretty good, likely due to her steady diet of American films and music. She dreamed of moving to Los Angeles someday and becoming a famous rock star. She made sure to read everything that she could about the Western entertainment industry, always keeping up to date on the latest trends, and practised on her guitar every day. Each week, her hair was a different colour. This week, it was bright pink. She was envious of Casey's natural red locks and found it curious that he lacked a single freckle.

"You are not afraid, are you?" She teased her companion. She regretted the comment instantly. Casey's face split into a smile, but it held no humour. She had seen him wear that smile often. It was a barbed-wire fence around his heart.

"What for?" He asked. "It's open to the public."

Kitty said nothing, but gave him a smile of her own. One filled with a gremlin's cunning. She led him around to the opposite side of the north tower. Once she was certain that the surrounding greenery shielded them from any prying eyes, she began searching the wall for her favourite hidden entrance. She had discovered it quite by accident during her night in the castle. Every so often, when she wished to be alone, she would use it to sneak back inside. Wewelsburg would then be her own private playground, a place where she was safe from the corruption of the outside world. With all the changes that were now going on within its walls, she wondered how much longer she would have its secrets all to herself.

The centuries old bricks bore the colour of cigarette ash and were formed so roughly that no two had the exact same shape. Kitty let her tiny fingers dance over the jagged rocks as she sought out one stone in particular. She looked forward to seeing Casey's reaction when she pushed it in and revealed a doorway which was hidden so cleverly that it had not been discovered in four hundred years. However, that hope was dashed when her companion managed to find it before her. Although he had never visited this castle before and had no knowledge of its history, the boy placed a soft palm in just the right place and unsealed the passageway. The side of the tower opened like a mouth and gaped before them.

Kitty was seriously beginning to wonder if Casey could not be psychic, for what she had just witnessed stretched her disbelief.

She led her chestnut-haired companion within and the door slid closed behind them, blending so well with the tower's wall that it was invisible to the untrained eye. The pair found themselves at the foot of a spiral staircase, which twisted upwards and out of sight through a narrow corridor. Long dead torches lined the sides. The only real illumination came from a few beams of fading sunlight which seeped through the cracks between the bricks. The lack of proper lighting made ascending the stairs difficult, even dangerous. It occurred to Kitty that if something happened to her here, the rest of the world might never find out about it. She would simply disappear unceremoniously from the face of the earth. She climbed the stairs carefully with Casey trailing close behind. Both took each step with care until they reached a marble platform, which Kitty always thought felt extravagant under her feet. Standing on it was like being someone special, so special that such a luxurious material

had been laid out just for her to step on. Perhaps there was a magic there too. Casey joined her on the elevated plane while she felt around in the dark for the next stage in their journey.

It must be here somewhere, she thought. Her hands landed on something round. A smile crept onto her lips as she took hold of the object and turned it. Reddish orange sunlight poured in on the interlopers as another hidden door opened in front of them, revealing Kitty's favourite spot in the entire castle.

The *Obergruppenführersaal*.

Above the front entrance to the room was a quote, *"Domus mea domus orationis vocabitur"*. Twelve beautiful windows, each one framed by dusty columns, formed a circle and poured the dusk's glow onto a strange symbol inscribed on the floor.

The mark of the Black Sun.

It was here that the magic was strongest. As green as Casey's eyes and no less haunted, the twelve-armed swastika charged the entire castle with its power. Kitty could feel it. She repressed a shudder as she entered the room. The air here was always still. Casey remained inscrutable as he followed her in. There was something unreal about him, something almost frightening.

"What are you thinking?" Kitty asked.

"I'm not sure." Casey answered. His mind seemed a million miles away, in a place she could neither reach nor fathom.

"What is this place?" He asked. Kitty grinned wickedly.

"The Nazis built this room." She explained. "Look out that window. Do you see that little house?"

"Yes." Casey replied.

"That is all that is left of Niederhagen concentration camp. The prisoners there were forced into slave labour and remodelled this castle according to Hitler's wishes. They say that he would sometimes gather the twelve highest ranking members of the SS in this room to practice the occult sciences. It is even said that their ghosts still haunt the vault below us."

Casey was silent. He stared hypnotized by the marble floor and the arcane seal that it displayed.

Green against white, just like his tortured eyes. Kitty wondered what was going through his head. If he was psychic, he was probably sensitive to whatever energies were filling the room. If he could feel them, then this was a moment she had prayed for. She watched in anticipation as he stepped towards the runic symbol as if in a trance. The mark of the Black Sun was calling to something deep inside him.

Something in his blood.

The second that his foot touched the occult pattern, the magical dimension thrust its gates open for Kitty to see. It began with a blue glow, which bathed the room in sapphire and made the girl feel as though she were beneath the ocean. Then came the smell. For the second time, Kitty's nostrils were invaded by the scent of bitter almonds. The stench was so strong that it threatened to choke her. Her lungs burned so badly that she found herself falling to the floor, gasping for air. Casey fixed his emerald eyes on her, but they wore an expression that did not belong to him. A power had filled him. It hardened his gaze beyond recognition, making it as cold as the Arctic Circle. He was like a man possessed. When he spoke, it was in a bizarre, gibberish dialect that Kitty did not recognize.

"Hwaz iuwiz?" He said.

"I don't understand." She answered in German. Casey's eyes narrowed coolly at the sound of her native tongue. A chill went up the girl's spine as her companion replied in a broken facsimile her own language.

"In seven hour, this boy become sixteen." Casey said in a voice that was not his. "His grandfather say that he then receive birthright. If you interfere, I cannot protect you. I warn you now, *fraulein*, and I only ever give one warning."

Kitty trembled as she listened to the superhuman entity which spoke through the boy's lips.

"Who are you?" She asked it. One corner of her companion's mouth curled upwards into a poison ivy smile. He giggled at her, like a taunting schoolgirl, then whispered a single word.

"Thule."

He crossed his arms in a bizarre salute.

"Goodbye, *fraulein*." He said. "Pray we not meet again. *Rahowa!*"

The glow from the twelve armed swastika faded, plunging the chamber into a mosaic of shadow and moonlight. Kitty hadn't even noticed that the horizon had claimed the sun for the night. She found herself able to breathe again as the poisonous smell returned to whatever realm it had emerged from. However, her red-headed friend collapsed to the floor like a puppet whose strings were cut. She waited for several seconds, afraid to approach the boy. But when he did not rise, concern overcame caution. She rushed to his side and pressed her fingers against his vulnerable throat. She was relieved to find a fairly strong pulse, yet his unconscious state lingered on. Kitty cradled Casey's head in her lap and studied his sleeping face with worry. He seemed so helpless now. She dared to stroke his copper hair while ruminating on her situation.

What should I do? She asked herself. She thought of calling an ambulance, but did not wish to find herself in trouble for adventuring into the castle after hours. She could picture her father's reaction, his scolding, his lecturing, not that she cared about it at this point. However, despite the sword which hung over her head, another question plagued her thoughts even further.

What is Thule?

Slowly, Casey opened his grassy eyes.

"W-what happened?" He asked groggily.

"You tripped and hit your head." Kitty said. She knew that it was unfair to lie to him. However, this was an opportunity which she had dreamt of for years and the prospects exhilarated her. The world of magic was all around her; in the wind, in the trees, in the lush green grass and the call of the birds. Most people would never see it, for it was invisible to the human eye. But it had been fantasized about since the dawn of evolution. Now, her own private window into this world was lying in her lap. Her personal, red-haired doorway to the mystical. She even knew when it would open next.

"Why did you not say that tomorrow is your birthday?" She asked. Casey retreated behind his fence.

"I didn't..." He began, but trailed off. Talking about it seemed to hurt him.

"You did not want to be a bother?" Kitty said. Her companion offered only a nod.

"How'd you find out?" He asked.

"Your mother told me." She lied again. His expression turned sour and the barbed wire wove itself between them, forming a barrier as impassable as prison walls. Kitty suspected that Casey had specifically asked his mother not to tell her about his birthday.

Before either of them could say another word, the room was filled by a dazzling light. Kitty shielded her eyes to keep from being blinded. She saw two silhouettes standing in the entrance, one of whom clenched a flashlight in its tight fingers.

"I thought I heard voices." The light bearer said. Casey's emerald eyes fell in shame.

"Hi, Mom." He said.

Mrs Morgan glared at her son in disapproval. It was startling how a woman so small could hold so much power over anyone, let alone a boy as tall and enigmatic as Casey. Her curly, raven hair and dark eyes had a way of making her appear rather witch-like. It did not even seem to matter how little time she spent in the sun, her too-natural-to-be-natural tan always stayed painted on her skin. These features combined made Kitty wonder if Casey was not bound into submission to his mother through some enchantment rather than his upbringing. Behind her stood an almost impossibly tiny man whom Kitty recognized immediately, for it was her own father. She should have guessed that he would be prowling about Wewelsburg Castle at night, since he was assisting Casey's mother with the proposed renovations.

"Don't 'Hi, Mom' me." Mrs Morgan sneered at her son. "What are you two doing here after closing time?"

"Please, do not blame Casey." Kitty interrupted. "The fault is mine. I thought I would frighten him by bringing him here and telling him *spukgeschichte*."

"Ghost stories." Her father translated.

"I did not mean for him to get in trouble." Mrs Morgan studied Kitty coldly. Those narrow, sorceress eyes shifted to the girl's father as the mind behind them took its time forming an opinion. But when that icy glare fell upon the mark of the Black Sun, the eyes widened in horror. Mrs Morgan began to fume.

"Come on, Casey." She said. "Let's go back to the hostel."

She grabbed her son by the wrist and pulled him to his feet. Kitty was not sure, but she thought that Mrs Morgan might have pulled a little too hard, for she felt Casey flinch as he was lifted from her lap. She watched as her companion, her red-haired doorway, was taken beyond her reach. She could not let that happen, not when she had come so close to touching the magic. She had to make a stand now.

"Please, Mrs Morgan." Kitty called after them. "Do not be angry."

Casey's mother ceased in mid-stride and fixed the girl with a lethal stare.

"You have no idea what you almost did." She snapped. Mrs Morgan stormed off into the night with her son in tow.

Kitty felt terrible. She hoped that the boy would not land in too much trouble. Her father remained silent, but gave her a drive back into the village. Thankfully, the old man was not angry at her. He was never angry with her, merely disappointed. She had tested that patience many, many times. Yet, for all their arguments, for all the enmity which passed between them, her efforts only ever won her more of his disappointment. As soon as she was beneath the red roof of her own home, she sought to put some distance between herself and the old man. Kitty locked herself in her bedroom and called up all of her friends. She decided that if her red-haired doorway was going to open tomorrow, then she would be ready to greet whatever came through it. She told her entire social circle that she was going to be throwing a party. She wanted to make sure that Casey had a sixteenth birthday to remember.

Once all of her plans were set in motion, she scoured the web in search of a single word. Much to her surprise, it turned out to be quite common and she read its meaning eagerly.

Thule (Too-Lah):

***

At that exact same moment, her red-haired doorway to the mystical lay shaking with terror in his room at Wewelsburg Youth Hostel. Casey and his mother had the suite all to themselves. Their own private killing jar. He rubbed the fresh bruises that she had planted upon his arm. It would be hours before they stopped stinging. They were Mrs Morgan's way of enforcing her rules, of hammering home the knowledge that she was in charge. He counted his lucky stars that they were not as bad as that one time when she had taken a hot iron to his cheek. He'd almost lost an eye then.

How many mothers raise their sons to hate themselves? He wondered. He knew that Rebecca Morgan was not the only violent parent walking the earth. He also knew what response he would receive if he ever sought escape from her shadow. He could hear the world think it.

Suck it up, buttercup.

Casey did not know why he could sometimes sense what others were thinking. His father and sister had both possessed the same gift. They used to treat it like a game. But his mother found it terrifying. She told him that he was unnatural and disgusting. Under her watch, he was forbidden from using his special gift or allowing anyone else to even know of its existence. So he kept it buried inside himself, surrounded by a deadly, barbed wire fence. To let it out for any reason would earn him his mother's wrath.

He relaxed himself by holding his favourite shell to his ear and listening to the sea. He had read that it was only a legend that the ocean could be heard through a seashell. Scientifically, it should be impossible for the sound of waves roaring upon the beach to reach him. Yet, he could hear those waves as clearly as spoken words.

Perhaps there was something special about this shell. Mrs Morgan had threatened to smash it many times, but never followed through on her intimidating words. Maybe she was afraid that she would have nothing left to threaten him with if she did. For that shell was the dearest thing to him in the whole world. It was something he had kept from those days by the ocean.

That last time he had seen his father and sister.

It was summer. The Morgans had rented a cottage on the seaside. One fine afternoon, Mr Morgan had taken little Megan out in the family boat while a ten-year-old Casey stayed onshore with his mother to help prepare dinner. Mrs Morgan was so different in those days, always ready with a smile for him. He used to cherish the time that they would spend together. She never judged him back then. She never hit him. Casey remembered being proud of the supper they had cobbled together from just a few, simple ingredients. They were both so excited. He could hardly wait for his father to taste it. But he did wait.

And he waited.

And he waited.

Night fell and he still waited. A search party eventually found the boat far out at sea, but there was no trace of his father or sister. It was as though the salt water had just swallowed them up. Every last ray of light disappeared from the Morgan family that day. This seashell was the only thing Casey had to remember any of it by. When Mrs Morgan put it to her ear, she heard nothing. But for him and him alone, the waves always had something to whisper. Sometimes, he could even hear his little sister laughing. Tonight, however, she was silent. He tried to picture Megan. If she was still alive, she would be thirteen now, developing an interest in boys and performing mischief to earn her mother's scorn. He attempted to imagine what sort of person she might have grown into.

Casey's tension unwound as he listened to the tide. He could feel it wash over him, draining away his anxiety and fear, stripping the colour from his soul. As the night wore on, he let himself doze off with the shell next to his ear. It is unsurprising, then, that he dreamed about the ocean.

And that one day.

He was standing on his father's boat as the waves slapped against the side. In his heart, he knew that that his family had to be on board somewhere. If he just searched hard enough, he could find them and the light would return to his household. His mother would smile at him again. He would never have any more bruises.

They had to be on this boat.

They just had to.

Casey searched from bow to stern, but found no trace of his father or his sister. The black waters rumbled, as if mocking him. He gazed into the endless deep, which had taken away all the happiness he had ever known. A mystery waited down there. Casey thought that he could solve it if he dared to dive far enough down. However, he was hesitant, for he did not know how deep was too deep. As defeat crept into his heart, the strange scent of bitter almonds descended on him. He saw a figure reflected in the water. At first, he thought it had to be Megan and his heart raced in excitement. But he soon realized that the veiled woman who appeared amongst the scrying waves was much too old to be his missing sister. She seemed dressed as though she was on her way to a funeral, in a wide, black hat with a dark cloth covering her face. She beckoned to him with long, curved fingernails while gently humming an operatic trill.

Suddenly, darkness filled the water. Twelve shadows, each one with a human posture, stretched out from the cryptic reflection. The ocean turned black as they encompassed the infinite waves and eclipsed every living thing within them.

"Join our tribe." The living darkness said. "Fight our war. Share our glory."

Casey awoke slowly, unsure if he was still in a dream. The moonlight seeping through the window cast strange shadows, making it appear as though his room were haunted. One in particular caught his eye. On the wall above his bed was a silhouette that resembled a human figure, standing over him like a nocturnal guard. Then, before he could make heads or tails of it, the shadow was gone. Had it been a vision? A ghost? Casey wondered if his gift allowed him the power of prophecy.

When he lay back down, there was something hard and lumpy under his pillow. He reached beneath the headrest and what he found made his heart tremble. It was a black dagger with a silver eagle embossed on the handle. In its claws, the bird of prey clutched a swastika, as if daring to carry it to greater heights. On the blade was an inscription.

Mein ehre heisst true.

Curiously, the dagger smelled of almonds.

Chapter 2

"There are two types of morals, those for the master and those for the slave. 'Master Morality' focuses on the individual's own happiness and well-being; all that benefits the self is good, all that takes from one's own person is bad. In 'Slave Morality', the reverse is true; self-sacrifice for the welfare of others is noble and honourable, but to seek thine own prosperity is greedy and corrupt. Give of thyself and you too shall find joy.

Surely the swiftest method of attaining control must be to follow the wisdom of Master Morality privately while preaching the virtues of Slave Morality openly. In this manner, others are convinced to work for the benefit of one who thinks only of benefiting their own self."

-Translated from Efeu's private journals

Nobody would ever accuse Otto Maurer of being strong-willed. The small man was notoriously timid by nature, with large eyes that would often widen in fear from behind his thick glasses and a brow which broke into a cold sweat at the first sign of conflict. It always amazed anybody that such a man could have attained the position of director at Wewelsburg Castle. He seemed to be more the type to be taking directions instead of giving them. But, as it stood, he was the director and in charge of running all aspects of the castle's day-to-day functions.

Which also meant that every problem was his to address.

His cellphone had remained blessedly silent all morning. However, as the noon hour descended upon him, he could not help but feel a presence hovering over his shoulder. Otto made a quick scan of his workspace and convinced himself that the sensation was just his imagination. However, it still made him uneasy. Despite the bright, midday sun transmitting its rays through his office window, the shadows felt unnaturally heavy, as if something were residing within them. At the far end of the room, he could practically make out a human silhouette, like a phantom standing guard over him.

Maurer's forehead felt wet and, without further warning, his cellphone rang.

"Hello?" He said into the receiver. He was answered by a voice which he had heard many times before. A woman spoke to him in very poor German. He could never place her accent. However, if he had to guess, he would have thought that it came from the north.

"Look out window." She ordered. There was so much authority in her voice. Maurer wished to resist her commands. He really did. But some power forced him to obey. He gazed out his window and into the castle's courtyard. Parked below was a black Mercedes which hearkened back to a dark chapter in Wewelsburg's history. His body shook at the sight of it, fearful of what he knew waited inside. From the backseat, he could sense a blue eye staring right through him.

"We want the *Obergruppenführersaal* tonight." The voice continued. "Make arrangements."

Maurer attempted to answer, but found his throat too dry. He swallowed what spit he could and choked up the necessary words.

"Yes, *fraulein*."

The line went dead and he put his cellphone down with a trembling sigh. He knew that he should not obey that sinister voice. But the memory of what had happened to his predecessor haunted him. After all, he'd been the one who had found the man's body, its eyes bulging, its face purple and barbed-wire wrapped tightly around its neck. It had all happened in this very office. The door was locked from the inside, but even that had not protected the former director from his assassin.

As the dead man's successor, Maurer lived in constant fear for his life. He knew that the voice was responsible for the murder, but was totally powerless against its owner. Her will was simply too strong. Once, he had found the courage to refuse her demands. He'd then returned home to find that his dog had been poisoned.

Maurer wiped the dampness from the top of his head and called his receptionist.

"Klaudia, have security meet me in my office." He instructed. "I have special duties for them tonight."

"Yes, *Herr* Maurer." The receptionist answered. The director of Wewelsburg Castle rubbed his eyes in exhaustion. He cast his gaze to the far end of the office. The shadowy sentry was gone, content that the *Obergruppenführersaal* would be free.

Nobody would ever accuse Otto Maurer of being strong-willed.

Which meant that he was the perfect man for his position.

Chapter 3

*"**The theory and practical use of romantic commodities;** The birth of democracy has spawned a paradoxical dilemma. Although every individual is, in theory, given a voice, these voices must be streamlined into a majority vote in order for the system to function. The individual voter is forced to choose which of their values are most precious to them and compromise all others in its name. Through the aid of runelore, the tribes have found a method for consolidating the voters' opinions in their favour. Just as a predator grooms its intended victim for abuse, a movement similarly grooms its victims for recruitment. They seek out the lost and lead them further astray with empty promises. For, in a democratic society, a tribe does not actually need to fulfill its proposed goals in order to win the fight. It only needs to acquire members.*

This process has three aspects; (1) 'Join our tribe', where the collective tells its audience a glossy version of who it is and what its values are. (2) 'Fight our war', where they discuss the challenges they face and identify their enemies. Typically, all of these enemies will be generalized as being a part of one larger sum (otherwise, the listener will begin to wonder how it is that the tribe can be right and everyone else can be wrong). (3) 'Share our glory', the aspect that often wins the most recruits. This is where the tribe tells its audience what they get out of the deal and describes vague, long-term goals. Here is where runelore comes into play. Understand that words and symbols serve the same purpose. They are both conveyors of ideas. Thus, in the art of runelore, words are effectively spoken runes. The incantations uttered by the tribe shall be what are commonly called 'glittering generalities'; freedom, duty, peace, strength, love, truth, God, equality, justice, progress, association with a revered historical figure (prestigious names make the most effective armour), patriotism, independence, rebellion, supremacy (be it racial, moral, intellectual, etc) and all the other romantic yet ultimately ambiguous ideas which admirals preach to convince children to march in front of them. They are words that appeal to emotions, but have unclear definitions. Whatever humanity romanticizes becomes perceived as having a high value, regardless of its practical worth. Consequently, everything with a high value comes into high demand. By exploiting the romantic nature of these glittering generalities, the tribe transforms them into something that can be capitalized upon. Abstract ideas then become commodities, which may be offered in exchange for the individual's allegiance. The runic formula for this is as follows:

Eh=Fa+Yr+Sig

*'Fa' (fire generation) represents the task that the speaker wishes for the audience to perform. 'Yr' (rainbow) is an emotional appeal which overrides the listener's ability to reason. 'Sig' (victory) is the 'romantic commodity' being offered (**Note:** often 'Yr' and 'Sig' can be compounded as one. For maximum effectiveness,*

'Sig' should always be something beautiful and 'Yr' should stroke the listener's ego). 'Eh' (marriage) is the audience's compliance.

For example, imagine that I made the statement that 'Group X' is better than 'Group Y' because it is more intelligent. 'Agreeing with my statement' would be the task I'd desire from my listener. In return, I'd be offering them a feeling of 'being intelligent' (by virtue of identifying with 'Group X'). That romantic commodity would also double as an emotional appeal (for the knowledge of one's own intelligence makes one feel good). Then, by complying with my desired task, they receive the impression of having made the smart choice. In short, I'd have bought their allegiance by offering them the illusion that agreeing with me makes them clever.

However, the above example only demonstrates this effect in the short term. For long term uses, consider this next scenario. Imagine that I have employed a group of volunteer workers and told them that what they are doing for me helps to end a war between two rival nations. The emotional appeal would be a feeling of contributing towards a noble cause. I might even make a second such appeal by showing them images or descriptions of the horrors of this war. My workers would then feel like heroes for helping to end such atrocities. 'Peace' would be the romantic commodity, offered in exchange for their volunteer work (which would, naturally, be the task). However, the moment that the conflict between the identified nations was resolved, the specific type of peace I've proposed would lose its value. When you have something, you don't need a merchant to supply it to you. With peace now in their hands, my employees would no longer have any incentive to perform volunteer work for me. An alternate scenario might have been that instead of a war between two rival nations, their duties contributed towards a generalized idea of 'peace'. The task and emotional appeal(s) would remain the same, but the romantic commodity would be defined in such a vague manner that the struggle to produce it would be perpetual. One conflict might end, but as long as more could be perceived as existing, 'peace' would still not be attained. If I kept making the emotional appeal(s) and the volunteer workers allowed their feelings to override their reason, they would then continue to perform my desired tasks indefinitely. Thus, they would strive endlessly for a dream that could not be fulfilled. A carrot that is always just out of reach.

On a private note, never trust a tribe that has advertised the same goals for more than two decades. They are either failures (since they have made no headway in all that time) or liars who are merely attempting to generate a pretense of high concept in the mind of the consumer in order to disguise the quality, or lack thereof, in the actual product.

Personal reminder: *Find the time to identify as many romantic commodities that appear in my own life as I possibly can."*

-Translated from Efeu's private journals

"If you'd told me that you were throwing this party for Casey, I never would've come."

Kitty could not believe the words that spilled from her best friend's mouth. Nor could she believe the spite with which Sarah Lin spoke them. The two girls had known each other since kindergarten, had grown up together and even dyed each others' hair. Kitty could not count how many times that the purple streak which ran through Sarah's silky, black hair had rested on her shoulder while her surrogate sister cried her eyes out. Neither could she put a number to the occasions on which that same sister's house had served as a sanctuary from more of her father's disappointment. Yet, despite these years of harmony, Kitty now found herself staring at her dearest friend as though she were a stranger.

"He's not that bad." Kitty defended. "He's just quiet."

"He's creepy." Sarah replied. "I can't stand the way he looks at me."

"He's shy, I can understand that." Kitty said. "Please, won't you give him a chance... for me?"

Sarah remained silent for a long time while her best friend waited anxiously to hear her answer.

Casey, on the other hand, felt that he had already heard everything he needed to. Sarah Lin's toxic thoughts burned his brain like acid. No matter how hard he tried to drown out the sound with his hands, nothing seemed to block the venom which had escaped her lips.

He's creepy.

It did not matter that she had spoken those words in another language. He had heard her with his gift and ideas always mean the same thing regardless of how they are phrased. Casey's only defence was the barbed-wire. He imagined a long, sharp fence between himself and every other living thing. It was impossible to climb, impossible to shatter, the perfect shelter. The cloud of emotion was pushed back, letting him breathe once again. However, the same poisonous sentiments emanated off of all the other party guests. Casey did not recognize a single one of the many teenagers who littered the small house. They were Kitty's friends, not his. To them, his presence at his own party was merely a formality to be tolerated. His birthday was nothing more than an excuse to gather and make merry. And make merry they did, yet he could sense that they would have been much merrier if he were not there. Casey's green eyes shifted from one face to the next and pictured his razor-like barrier blocking each and every one of them off. Although the cloud of their feelings hovered just outside, it remained there and failed to taint his own thoughts. Now that he was safely fortified, he could think about blending in. Natural selection; the strongest survive by adapting to their hostile environment. Casey arranged his face so that it betrayed no thoughts, ideas or pain. It was a perfect mask.

Show no weakness, he told himself. Keeping his disguise in place, he navigated through the thick atmosphere. He avoided eye contact on his journey, ensuring that he would not to provoke any unwanted confrontations. Casey reached the kitchen without any disturbances, but was annoyed to find someone else already there. An elegant woman, much older than any of the teenaged guests, was leaning against the counter with her arms crossed. She looked to be in her late thirties, if not older, and was dressed in a smart business suit with her blond hair up in a bun. On her right hand, she wore a ring of the finest silver, decorated with Nordic runes and a morbid death's head. He was suspicious of the smile she gave him as he opened the refrigerator and searched for something sweet to drink.

"You're Casey, aren't you?" The woman asked. The birthday boy nodded as he poured himself a glass of root beer. He noticed that she spoke English much better than anyone else he had met in this country. Even her accent was barely noticeable.

"Happy Birthday." She continued. "Are you enjoying the party?"

Casey drank his soda quickly and gave her a second nod.

"You're lying." The woman said with a knowing smile. "I can tell. You're not happy at all, are you?"

Casey eyed her and felt nervous. Something about this lady was setting off an air raid siren in his skull. He relaxed the barbed wire a little and attempted to read her thoughts. She possessed a lot of anger, but it was not directed at him. No, she appeared to feel nothing but admiration for him. He could not fathom why. However, there was another presence in her mind. A force of some sort, as if God were poking his almighty finger into an ant farm. Casey saw a blue eye looking back at him from inside her brain. An eye which somehow knew everything about the boy. An eye that saw right through him. Casey didn't know what it was or where it came from. He told himself that he didn't want to know, but he knew that he was lying. The eye knew it too.

"Are you Kitty's mother?" He asked. The living enigma before him shook her head.

"I wasn't even invited." She said. "I just came to see you. I've been waiting to meet you for a long time."

To meet me?

Casey froze up. Every muscle in his thin frame clenched as she stepped towards him. He could sense that arcane force rising off of her like an almond musk. It reached towards him and scratched at his fence with wicked talons, clawing its way through the barbed wire with a deadly effectiveness. He shrank from the power emanating from her, terrified that such a force could exist. Terrified that it could touch him so easily. Terrified that its will could be so much stronger than his own.

"Don't be afraid." The woman said. "My name is Lucy and I represent a... a sort of a club. It's very, very old. Your grandfather was a member many years ago and he left instructions that, when you turned sixteen, you were to be offered a place in our humble group."

She gave him a mephistophelian smile.

Join our tribe.

"You're sixteen today. We're throwing a party too. Would you like to come?"

"Where?" Casey asked suspiciously.

"The castle." She said. "My car is waiting outside."

Casey felt that superhuman will calling to him. Beckoning him.

Join our tribe.

"I-I don't think that would be a good idea." He said. The boy rejected the force's desires with every atom in his being. Fresh acres of barbed wire stretched between Lucy and himself, pushing that occult willpower away. He turned from his blond Mephistopheles and headed towards the door. But the eye still stared into him from beyond the fence.

"Have you ever wondered why you sometimes know what other people are thinking?" Lucy called after him. "Telepathy is a rare gift. We know why you have it. Would you like to know too?"

"Sorry." Casey answered without breaking his stride. "Not interested."

"Would you be interested in seeing your father and sister again?"

Casey froze in his tracks. The foundations of his barrier began to shake and crumble. The barbed wire rusted. He turned around anxiously and faced this strange, riddle-born woman.

"What have you done with them?" He asked. He wasn't sure if it was a demand or a plea.

"We haven't done anything." Lucy replied. "They're perfectly happy, except that they both miss you terribly."

Share our glory.

Casey felt the alien will tear his fence asunder and hook its claws into his soul. It pulled at him with inhuman strength. Pulled him towards the eye.

Join our tribe.

Fight our war.

Share our glory.

His own eyes narrowed in intrigue.

"What sort of club did you say this was?"

Lucy grinned diabolically.

"We are called *Das Thule Gesellschaft*, or 'Thule Society' in English." She explained. "It has been around for a long time and was founded on some of this country's most ancient traditions. But come, there is someone who can explain it all much better than me, someone who has waited decades for this day."

She held out her hand, as if offering him a dance. Casey remained hesitant. Lucy's fingers almost seemed to beckon him. Her palm was a contract awaiting his signature. In return, it offered answers, a peek behind the curtain to see the wizard at work. For there was a wizard there, someone with a gift similar to his own, whose mental powers were strong enough to tug at him from afar.

Someone who had been waiting to meet him since before he was born.

Share our glory.

Casey pushed his hesitation aside and accepted Lucy's hand. That same hand led him from the room. It pulled him away from his peers, away from his own party. He was a ship drifting from the fleet. Drifting towards what? The only way for him to learn was to remain adrift and see where the current led. The exit appeared before him amidst the sea of adolescence. If he followed his personal Mephistopheles through it, he knew that he could not return. It would mean severing his final ties to this youthful tribe.

It would mean that he no longer cared what Kitty thought.

Kitty. Casey's only friend amid the tribe was searching frantically for him. Her pink hair stood out like a beacon from the desert of sameness. One word was printed in rainbow letters on her black top.

Freedom.

Freedom for her perhaps, but not for him. As much as he appreciated all of the preparations she had made for his birthday, her world was simply not his. For a brief instant, her brown button eyes met his emeralds and he wished that he could take her with him. But it was not meant to be. His green jewels fell from her gaze and the barbed-wire cut her off from him for good.

Lucy opened the door and, making a choice that he could never undo, Casey stepped through.

A vintage Mercedes, polished to an immaculate shine, was parked on the curb, waiting for them to climb inside. Casey had never dreamed of being chauffeured in such a luxurious coach. This in itself was a birthday present. He sat himself in the backseat while Lucy took the wheel and started the engine. The ride proved relaxing and enjoyable. The seats were of cushioned leather and Casey thought it felt good to run his fingers over the surface. However, it also felt a little shameful, for God only knew how many cattle had been stripped of their hides to provide this sort of comfort to the human race. Perhaps it was the fate of lesser animals to be herded and exploited as livestock. However wrong it may seem, the reality remained that humanity needed to eat and no amount of shaming would ever change that. Does a fox ever stop to ponder the morality of slaughtering a rabbit? No, for doing so would mean its own starvation. If every fox gave of itself and went hungry for the well being of the poor little bunnies, its own species would go extinct from lack of nourishment. Thus, the foxes ate the rabbits while the humans ate the cows, drank their milk and used their skin as an accessory.

The horizon had turned a dusty collection of oranges and violets by the time that the Mercedes pulled up in front of Wewelsburg Castle. Lucy parked the car near the bridge by the eastern wall and they both got out to admire the ancient structure. With the sun setting behind it, the castle's shadow stretched forward like a pit. Although his chauffeur stepped into it without any hesitation, Casey felt uneasy. Somewhere inside that fortress, he sensed a presence. It was something that had plagued his nightmares ever since the day his father and sister disappeared. He had seen it in his mother's eyes every time she struck him. It was present in every bruise and cut with which she had decorated his body. In every scar she had ever left on his brain. When he cleared his mind, he could see the omniscient blue eye staring back at him from inside. It called to him, daring him to set foot in the world of the Black Sun.

Join our tribe.
Fight our war.
Share our glory.

He looked down at the pavement beneath his feet and saw that he was already standing on a shade of uniform grey. So, he lifted his boot and marched forward into the darkness. Lucy was waiting there for him, leaning her back against one of the great stone fixtures at the edge of the bridge. In years past, it had served as a shelter for the castle's guards. Now, it was just another decaying remnant of the Third Reich, with two defaced "Sig" runes above the door as the only visible sign of its former allegiance. Casey joined his driver in front of it, yet he remained transfixed by those twin lightning bolt symbols. It was the same fascination which he had felt the evening before. It awakened a strange feeling inside him, as if something in his blood was being touched. That same something was what drove him forward. It sickened, frightened and excited him all at once. He knew that he should feel nothing but horror at the atrocities of the Holocaust. He could see his mother's face now, glaring down on him in disapproval. In her hand, she held a hot iron.

I have tried to be tolerant, he thought. *I have tried to be accepting. I have tried to be everything you wanted me to be. But no matter what I did, I still remained the enemy.*

Casey was so hypnotized by the SS runes that he failed to notice that the woman leaning beneath them was not actually Lucy. One of the many vices of walking in the darker half is that the path is not always clear. Although she bore a striking resemblance to his chauffeur, enough to convince him that they were probably sisters, he could see the differences now that he was closer. While Lucy maintained a respectable appearance, her sibling appeared absolutely filthy. With short hair that looked as though it had not been washed in ages and a worn out leather jacket, her utterly trashy image was finished by a tight mini skirt and faded top with the same death's head design as Lucy's ring.

The blond Mephistopheles herself waited on the opposite side of the iron door, practically invisible in the evening shadow. As Casey approached, he found that even their attitudes towards him contrasted one another. While Lucy attempted to allure him through comfort, her twin made no secret out of her hostility. When he came near, she grumbled something in German. Something that did not sound the slightest bit welcoming.

"Speak in English in front of him." Lucy snapped.

"You know that this is our safe space." Her broken mirror image snorted with contempt. "He should not be brought in."

Casey halted in his tracks. He could sense that this woman had a barbed-wire fence of her own. His eyes studied her putrid form. She disgusted him in every way. From her stringy hair, to the fowl smell that rose off of her, she was like some wretch that wasted its days laying in the gutters and washed its problems away with a bottle of cheap wine.

Something degenerate.
Something subhuman.
Untermensch.

For a moment, Casey heard the word in his mind, but was uncertain if he was thinking it towards her or if she was thinking it towards him. However, Lucy remained unfazed by her sibling's remarks.

"The *fraulein* wishes for him to be present." She responded with a note of scorn. "Tell me, Kikka, would you want to be the one who informs her that it should be otherwise?"

Kikka's face warped into a mask of malice. Casey could sense the raw hatred seeping out from her. Its toxicity burned at him, compelling him to reinforce his own fence. A border of feelings became clearly marked between them, dividing them by many layers of barbed-wire, until reconciliation became impossible. The line was drawn and both sides knew where they stood.

"Well, far be it from me to go against our beloved *fraulein's* wishes." Kikka snorted. "Just remember, I was the one who said it first."

Lucy ignored her twin with her head held high. Never giving Kikka a second glance, she opened the gate-like door of the guard post and motioned for Casey to follow her inside. He eyed the dirty woman nervously as he slipped by her and she eyed him right back. Her two sapphires reminded him of a picture he had seen once. It was of a soldier who suffered from post traumatic stress disorder.

Such haunting eyes...

In front of him, Lucy opened one of Kitty's secret doors and a soft breeze escaped from the other side. Casey thought it smelled like almonds. He followed his chauffeur through the opening as Kikka stalked from a safe distance behind him. The idea of getting close to him appeared to repulse the filthy vagabond, so she merely dogged their steps with a sulk. Perhaps it was for the best that she did. Casey was not sure if he could have stood her stench if she came any closer. His chauffeur led them down a set of stone steps to a passage that appeared to trail off into nothingness. A few torches provided light from their mounts upon the grey brick walls. But even their glow seemed dimmer the further down they went. It was almost as if the tunnel led into the abyss itself. As he walked through it in silence, Casey wondered what sort of counter-culture would gather in the castle of the Black Sun? The answer, of course, was perfectly clear. That same cocktail of revulsion and excitement bubbled up again in his stomach. He sensed that azure eye again and the willpower that it projected. As its hold on him became stronger, he pictured the apparition from his dream squeezing him in a maternal embrace. Her hold made the revulsion fade and the

excitement grow. His mother's disapproving glare faded, until it was a mere shade.

For all my efforts, I am still the enemy. If I am unworthy of her love, why should she be worthy of mine? Why should any of them?

The prospect of shedding his skin lured him further, like a light at the end of a tunnel.

The light is good, he heard an unknown voice whisper softly in his mind. *Go towards the light.*

Casey found himself racing ahead of his guide. He no longer needed Mephistopheles. He knew the way on his own now. Even in the pitch blackness, he knew the way. He ran through the maze of darkened catacombs, guided by pure instinct.

Join our tribe.

Fight our war.

Share our glory.

Casey bolted up the same staircase which Kitty had shown him the day before. Without even trying to find it, his hand fell on something round. By turning it, he opened the secret door to the *Obergruppenführersaal.* As he stepped into the moonlit room, he had to admit that he was rather disappointed. No swastika banners hung from the ceiling. No generals in period costumes had come to salute a long gone Fuhrer. The chamber appeared deserted, save for the shadows.

The shadows.

As his eyes adjusted, he saw strange shapes cast upon the walls. They resembled human figures dressed in long robes with tall, pointed hoods. They were a part of the gloom itself. Every patch of shade, every piece of the abyss, was a living, breathing entity. It parted as he approached, as if he were a Nazi Moses being allowed passage into the promised land. But as the sea of living darkness split itself, it revealed a secret in its depths. Beneath the blackened surface lurked a creature. Not a shadow, but she who commanded the ebony waves.

Casey Morgan was standing in the presence of the Thule Society's ivory-carved idol.

Chapter 4

"The ancient art of runelore is sacred to my

people. In its classical form, it is our spiritual link to the faith of our ancestors. This practice is neither witchcraft nor superstition, but a discipline for the self. Each of the Nordic runes possesses its own unique meaning. By wearing them as symbols on our uniforms and banners, they act as subliminal commands, prompting their bearers to adopt the higher qualities that they represent unconsciously. There is nothing 'supernatural' about it at all, it is mere autosuggestion. For one who possesses our psionic 'gift', runelore acts as an aid for tapping into the subconscious, magnifying one's talents in the process. But even without these abilities, the practice remains valid as a methodology towards personal empowerment. The solo practitioner might even assign new meanings to the runes and the legitimacy of the discipline would not be compromised.

What follows is a list of those runes which are considered the most divine in my Fatherland, as well as their respective interpretations.

__Fa:__ Generation through fire, like the phoenix rising from its own ashes. Fire, by its very nature, represents destruction and the ability to build from destruction requires a special strength. Thus, only the weak mourn their losses. The strong rebuild their lives from the ground up.

__Ur:__ A symbol of the primordial and the secrets it contains. A doorway to introspection and reflection, for self-knowledge is self-mastery.

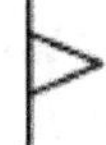

__Thorn:__ The spear of Odin. The lance which pierced Christ's side. The weapon that brings destruction so that renewal may occur. The old songs describe it as particularly baneful to women.

__Os:__ Power through the spoken word. A blessed sign not only for priests and writers, but for warriors as well. Words are the vessels of ideas and through our words we fight upon the psychic plane. To overcome enemy forces, conquer their minds. Lay claim to their land by winning the allegiance of their people. In this manner, we fight to sway opinion in our favour. We never cease speaking despite being silenced with the label of 'hate speech'. By exploiting this vague concept, by saying 'this is hate' and 'that is not', the enemy controls what may or may not be said. They expose themselves as paranoid tyrants, afraid of words. But empowered by the Os rune, we see the strength which lies in our voices. We break free of the enemy's quieting fetters and teach ourselves to grow more proficient in the craft of dictation. For if our foes are enraged by the words we speak, that only serves as a sign that we are doing our jobs.

__Rit:__ The sign of faith in oneself. This rune fills you with unshakeable confidence in your own methods. It teaches us that human perception, by the very nature of perception, can never be objective. Whosoever seeks to prove a theory shall inevitably succeed. Whoever seeks to disprove that same theory shall also succeed. The idea that either person is thinking objectively is just another romantic commodity. Despite claims to the contrary, humanity has yet to invent a 'good' system. All we have are systems on which we can coast temporarily until they self-destruct. Thus, with no objectively 'good' philosophy, one individual will live by one rule and another by their own. So, when our enemies tell us that we are wrong and must be 'fixed', we shall be able to tell them with total conviction 'I am my own person, you have no right to change me'.

__Ka:__ A branch of the great tree of life, Yggdrasill. It stretches out from its base, reminding us of the importance of our own seeds

spreading from our beings. Your children are the most precious of all your possessions. A rune to breed wisdom in nurturing one's family.

Hagal: *Knowledge that the god of your race lies not without, but within his people. Churches, ministries and covens all exist solely to trick you into putting your faith in their hands instead of your own. God might have created humanity, but it was humanity who created religion. To find God, one needs to search no further than their own heart.*

Not: *The rune of fate. Past and future are inescapably entwined, for nothing happens without a cause. This symbol will aid the search for the source of an occurrence. Once the cause is understood, the effect may be predicted. This power of prediction then grants you mastery over your own fate, rather than letting fate be your master.*

Is: *Ice, which represents coldness. The power to remain unaffected by outside influences. A symbol of fortitude.*

Ar: *The sun's ability to cast away the darkness. A protective rune against negative thoughts and emotions.*

Sig: *The symbol of victory! It shows us the light at the end of the tunnel. Not just a reminder of everything we are fighting for, but also a push to keep up the fight.*

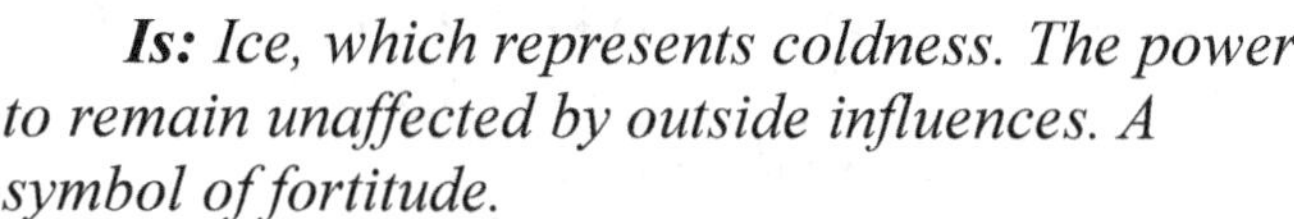

Tyr: *The immortality sign. Every one of us touches the lives of those around us in ways that we cannot fathom. Through them, our memory and influence lives well beyond our own deaths. A good life will leave a legacy that survives for many mortal lifetimes. A great life shall be immortal. Herein lies the significance of the Tyr rune; do not fear death, it cannot kill you.*

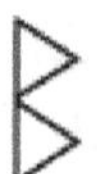

Bar: *The cycle of life, from the womb to the pyre. The circumstances of our lives are beyond our control. There shall be great joys as well as great perils. When these perils come is decided by a power greater than us. Our place is not to grieve over their coming, but to survive them. Any peril can be either a barrier or a stepping stone. The difference is entirely up to us.*

Laf: *The rune of science. It tells us to read the map before beginning our journey.*

Eh: *The wedding mark, linked inseparably to Ka. As your children are to be treasured above all else, select the person with whom you wish to create them very carefully. Remember that they will be your spouse's offspring too. Your bloodline will be shaped by the both of you. Seek a companion, not a plaything. Search for a nurturer, not one who wishes to be nurtured. A rune to inspire wisdom in the realm of romance.*

The Wolf's Angel Cross: *A symbol of supreme divinity and its bond with the human race. This divinity is not some distant, metaphysical being. It lives through cause and effect, physics and biology, natural selection and evolution. To attain the meaning of this rune is our ultimate goal; to evolve beyond our limitations into something greater than ourselves. Thus, to all the worshippers of equality, the high priests of democracy and the Legion of the*

Average do I issue this warning; beware of evolution! The assumption that you are a finished product, that life as you understand it must be the highest form in existence, is only classical human arrogance. It is so unthinkable that something can be just plain better than you, isn't it? So, I tell you to live in fear of the day that the Homo Sapiens take their next step. The first man to achieve evolutionary progress shall inevitably attain supremacy over his contemporaries. When he does, that shall be the day on which Nature, the most tyrannical of all dictators, selects you and your philosophy for extinction.

The Totenrune: *This rune warns of confusion and error. Often our enemies shall attempt to disorient us by exploiting our ability to feel emotion, especially pity, shame and guilt. I despise pity. I spit on it! It is the weapon of the weak. Many shall ask you for charity and protection. But when it is your neck in the noose, just try counting how many of these same wretches come riding to your rescue. Wear the Totenrune to protect yourself from these parasites. Have it engraved on your tombstone to warn others of your mistakes. It shall be a reminder that the key to a race's survival lies in abandoning the philosophy of compassion for the meek, which is based in the Hebrew scripture and is thus of Semitic origin, and embracing the only law which no force in existence has the power to repeal. The law which states that only the fittest survive.*

The Lebensrune: *A rune especially favourable to mothers, both biological and surrogate. It tells of how every mother assumes the role of the overman in the hearts of her children. She is the one who instills her values in the young, who teaches them what to believe and whose actions shapes their behaviour. Motherhood is a truly hallowed concept in my homeland. Whoever wins the allegiance of the world's mothers commands the future. Thus, the Lebensrune is both a blessing for women and a warning for men.*

If I may be permitted a personal note on this subject, I should like to add that if children cannot find love in their mothers' homes, we ought to expect that they shall seek it elsewhere. We also ought to expect that, since loveless homes make poor points of reference, they will begin this search in all the wrong places."
-Translated from Efeu's private journals

The sun had vanished over the horizon and Rebecca Morgan was pacing nervously from one end of the killing jar to the other. She was thankful to the castle's administration for granting her and Casey their own private space in the youth hostel. However, she still felt ill at ease. Somehow, she just knew that something was happening to her son. Perhaps it was her maternal instincts. Or maybe the boy was trying to warn her with that freakish ability of his. Once, the idea might have touched her. The mysterious nature of that gift was part of what had drawn her to his father all those years ago. But now, the mere idea terrified her. She knew the origin of that power and she wanted it out of her brain. She wanted her mind to be her own.

I never should have given birth, she thought. Children had seemed like such a good idea once upon a time. But now the boy was an anchor chained to her womb. With each day, as his father's features crept into his face, she saw him less and less as a son and more as a... *thing*. She woke up every morning and dreaded what he might become someday. She knew that it was wrong to hit a child. But what choice did she have, knowing the monster that he could easily grow into? He needed to be controlled. He needed to be disciplined.

Before he hurt somebody.

The soft, relaxing sound of waves roaring on the beach reached Mrs Morgan's ears. Its familiarity made her freeze in terror.

She recalled that last day by the ocean.

The noise led her to Casey's corner of the suite. One would expect a boy's space to be filled with a boy's things. However, her son had done nothing to liven up the room in the month that he'd spent living in it. His little nook remained exactly as it had appeared the day he'd first moved in. Even the same cheap pine scent was still hanging in the air. If it were not for the crumpled bed-sheets and the suitcase on the floor, she would have had trouble believing that the room was ever occupied at all.

And then there was the seashell.

That accursed relic of happier days lay next to his pillow. She had told him to get rid of it on several occasions, but he absolutely refused to part with the blasted thing. He had always told her that the ocean could speak to him through it. His voice would then tremble slightly, anticipating the slap that would sometimes follow, and his haunted, green eyes would arch downwards pitifully as if to say...

"Why don't you love me, Mommy?"

In those moments, he would stop being just a disgusting thing in her mind and start being a child. A son who needed guidance. A baby who needed to be taught right from wrong. A boy who wanted nothing more than his mother's approval. In those moments, she would cave in. So, Casey was allowed to keep his precious shell. Now, it wished to whisper its secrets to her, just as it whispered them to him.

Rebecca Morgan lifted Neptune's gift to her ear. Her apprehension seemed to vanish as the sound of waves soothed her. It was like a warm iron, easing the wrinkles from a damp cloth. For the first time, she truly understood how her son must feel about his most prized possession. It took her back to the days when her family was still together.

When she still had a husband who loved her.

And a daughter who wished to grow up to be just like her.

"We have him." The ocean said.

And it sounded just like little Megan.

The shell slipped from Rebecca Morgan's slender fingers as shock gripped her. She watched it shatter on the floor with wide eyes. The waves disappeared in an instant, leaving only a memory of the sea's voice.

And three frightening words.

We have him...

Relaxation was replaced by tension.

No, she thought, fighting back tears. *Not him too. How did they get to him?*

She tore through Casey's possessions. She searched through his suitcase, rummaged through his clothes, but found nothing out of the ordinary. Finally, under his mattress, she found the dagger. Mrs Morgan held it up to the light and read the inscription on the blade.

Mein ehre heisst true.

"My honour is called loyalty."

There was no question anymore. They had found him.

She tried calling her son on his cellphone, but knew that it was pointless. When he didn't answer, she ran to her own suitcase and spent several minutes rooting through it. Buried at the bottom was a faded envelope, a memento from her missing husband. Although it was intended for their son, she had broken the seal on it ages ago. Many times, she had dreamed of throwing it in the fireplace, thus freeing the boy from his family's legacy. Yet her hands had always proven too weak. As if compelled by a will that was infinitely stronger than her own, she had kept the letter safe all these years, waiting for the day when she felt courageous enough to hand it to Casey. It was this same will which had also drawn her to Wewelsburg, the last place on earth to which she should have brought her son. No matter how hard she tried, she was powerless to resist its allure. Every time it pressed itself upon her brain, she could feel an eye watching her back.

For the hundredth time, Rebecca Morgan opened the envelope. A strange, almond-like smell seemed to fill the room as she removed the letter's contents. Inside were several loose pages, hand-written in German with a number of strange illustrations. They depicted ancient rune symbols, like the vikings used to engrave on their swords and shields. Casey would not be able to understand a thing on those pages anyways. He'd never had the opportunity to learn his ancestral language, she had seen to that. But there was another item that disturbed her.

Sandwiched between two of the pages was an

old, black and white photograph. Dr Baldur Wolf, Casey's grandfather, was dressed sharply in a woollen tunic and matching pants. SS insignia glowed proudly on the collar and the edges of a swastika were just barely visible on his armband. He had a bucktoothed grin on his face and a death's head visor cap in his rough hands. Standing on either side of him were two recognizable figures. SS Reichsfuhrer Heinrich Himmler held his usual unassuming demeanour on the doctor's right side, while Karl Wiligut congratulated him on the left. Beneath this unholy trinity of the Third Reich's occult masters, there was a short message written in blue ink:

Thule-Gesellschaft – 04/30/1941, Zeit zeigt alles.

However, Rebecca's soul was always chilled less by what she saw in this picture than by what she should not be seeing in it. Hidden in the background, barely discernible through the sepia toned grains, was a fourth figure who did not belong there. Someone who shouldn't even exist.

A woman in a black veil.

Chapter 5

*"**Of the four virtues;** There are four ideals which are cherished in my Fatherland. These are race, creed, class and kind.*

***Race** is the most important of the virtues, for one's primary loyalties are always to their own people (familiarity being the first rule of attraction). This instinct does not exist by accident. It is a natural part of our beings and should be embraced. Remember that religions, political views, social classes, castes and philosophies can all die off and be resurrected later on. When a race dies, it is dead forever.*

***Creed** follows closely behind. Within our people's faith lies the foundations of our own unique culture. The foreigner's beliefs may appear more exotic, but never forget that his creed was developed to benefit his people. To follow his path should inevitably turn us against our own kin. Disbelief in your people's creed is a sign that you lack a connection with them. It is a fault in your character, not theirs.*

***Class** exists in even the most egalitarian societies. I dare you to show me one attempt to close the gap between the upper and lower bastions that did not result in a colossal failure. No, my friends, class is here to stay. Why does it exist at all? Because those at the top of the ladder came from stock that had the strength, cunning and merit to climb there. If you do not like that others lord over you, do not blame them. Blame your own ancestors, who proved too weak to rise to that same elitist position (and would have in a heartbeat if they'd only been strong enough to do so). My people openly reject the Marxist notion of 'internalized class struggle', which seeks to eliminate merit from the social playing field by claiming that all should have equal shares regardless of how much weight they actually pulled. Understand that if one does not make a distinction between that which is inferior and that which is superior, then nothing has value. Excellence cannot exist if it not contrasted against something lower. One should not fight against the class system, but aspire to gain the necessary qualities for rising within it. Class is a ladder and, just like any other, it can be climbed with the right amount of effort. Only recognize that in order to reach the top, you must push others to the bottom in the process.*

***Kind** is the final virtue and the one which binds all the others together. Like minds and people shall gravitate towards each other. Your kind can be many things. It can be your race. It can be your creed. It can be your views. Any policy that benefits your own kind is a good one. Any act which is detrimental to your kind is betrayal."*

*-**Translated from Efeu's private journals***

The Wewelsburg Youth Hostel had six corridors, each with its own showers. Unlike the rest of the castle, these shared bathing rooms had been redone in recent years and their new look stood out against the renaissance trappings.

Michelle really needed this shower. The cleansing rain washed away days worth of dirt and sweat. When had she last given herself a good scrubbing? It was back at that dingy motel in

Hamburg, the one that didn't even have hot water. Oh well, nobody ever said that backpacking across Europe for the summer would be easy. Fun, but not easy. She had already hit most of her major hot spots; London, Paris, Venice. Wewelsburg was just a slight detour on the road to Berlin. It wouldn't have even been necessary if that blasted truck driver hadn't blown an axle. He'd promised to take her straight through Paderborn. Promises, promises. Luckily, the hostel was just a couple of kilometres away. She had hiked it easily. It wasn't until she'd seen her room that she realized just how worn out she was.

But the shower helped.

The soft tinkling sound relaxed her and the warm, soapy water soothed her aching body. But a second sound reached her ears, one of a door creaking open. It didn't surprise her. After all, this was a shared shower. Michelle peaked out from behind the curtain and saw a pink haired girl enter the stall next to hers. Strange, the newcomer hadn't undressed. Did she intend to bathe with her clothes on? What struck Michelle as even stranger was that she never heard the water turn on in the next stall. She listened for it, but the sound didn't come. What she did hear was a low grating, like stone brushing against stone.

Did she dare to look to learn its source?

The thought of intruding on the other girl's privacy made her uncomfortable. However, curiosity won the day. Michelle poked her head around the corner and peered into the adjoining shower. As she had surmised, the water was not running. But a doorway was closing. She stared in awe at the secret passage. She did not know where it led, but something told her that she should not let it seal up again. Her duffel bag lay undisturbed on the wet, tiled floor. She raced towards it as the opening in the wall became smaller with each second. She grabbed hold of her gear, but felt that she simply could not make it back to the door in time. With each second, that black crack in the wall came closer to vanishing forever. Michelle shoved her duffel bag in the doorway, jarring it open just in time, and sighed in relief. She shut off her shower and dressed quickly. She was sopping wet, but she didn't care. Curiosity was pushing her

forward. Her adventurous spirit was just itching to see what secrets lay hidden behind the walls.

Michelle pulled open the secret panel and stepped through. Waiting on the other side was a long, torch-lit corridor, decorated with medieval statues on either side. As she walked between those stone relics, she could almost feel their grey eyes watching her. Who were they anyways? Forgotten knights? Soldiers from the crusades? The Ku Klux Klan?

Now what made her think of that? She studied the statues and recognized a Germanic cross engraved on their shields. The Iron Cross. Michelle repressed a shiver. Racism always made her feel uncomfortable. But, for some reason, the feeling was amplified here. The eyes of the statues dug into her wet flesh, as if they were haunted by fallen warriors. Inquisitors.

And where the hell was that pink-haired girl?

Michelle's question was answered by a shrill scream. It echoed down the corridor and through her body. Her heart pounded at the sound. Her feet pounded too. They beat heavily against the stone floor as she raced down the hall, down a maze of twists and turns.

Down into the old torture chambers.

She followed the scream to an iron door. She trembled before it. She knew that someone needed her help on the other side, someone who might be dying. But the door seemed to radiate a power that felt filthy on her skin. It made her wish that she was back in the shower. Softly, she placed her hand on the iron slab and pushed it open just a crack. Peeking through the opening, she gasped at what she saw beyond.

The pink-haired girl was there alright. She was tied to a wooden chair, but she was alive. Michelle thought that she looked so pitiful. So broken. She couldn't stand to see anybody like that, so she pushed the door open and raced inside. The room looked to be some kind of laboratory, but the sort that she would have expected to belong to Dr Frankenstein. A phrenology graph hung above a bookcase which held a collection of human skulls, each one labelled as belonging to a different racial type. Next to them lay a cadaver. At least, Michelle thought that the dissected mess was a cadaver. It had to be. Nobody could be cruel enough to do that to a human body while it was still alive. Strange medical instruments which she had never seen before were arranged about the lab and a small library sat in the corner. A quick scan of the books on display revealed that they were all written in runes. Michelle had no idea how to read runes, but recognized them as an ancient mystical alphabet. It was curious, then, that all the books looked brand new.

She rushed to the captive girl's side and got to work undoing her bonds. She noticed fresh needle marks on the poor thing's arms. Had she been drugged?

"Don't worry." Michelle said. "I'm gonna get you out of here."

The ropes proved easy to undo. But even though she was free, the girl's eyes remained glassy. Yet, behind their chemical daze, Michelle saw them fill with terror.

"The wall." The girl whimpered. Michelle followed her gaze and saw what she meant. Cast upon the wall was a human shadow, even though nobody stood in front of it. A shadow without a body. The shape wore a long robe with a tall klan hood. In its hand, it held a ceremonial dagger that glinted in the torchlight. A real dagger. Michelle had no idea how a shadow could be holding a real dagger. She opened her mouth to scream as the figure raised its weapon, but by then it was too late. Michelle's voice was cut off as the blade slit her throat.

<u>Chapter 6</u>

"In my social experiments, I have ascertained that within any tribe there are three basic types of tribesmen, none of whom make particularly flattering portraits. The first and most common type is the Hunter-Gatherer. Far more concerned with its own day-to-day survival, this individual possesses only a passing interest in the tribe's ideals. Most are born into their way of living and simply cannot imagine any other existence. To them, it is 'normal'. Others are lured into it with the promise that the chore of earning their daily bread shall be made easier. The Hunter-Gatherers are charged with the simplest task of all tribesmen; keeping their kind's bonfire burning with their support. By merely identifying as a member of the tribe, they validate it on the democratic stage. While effectively slaves to the other two types, they are, in some ways, also more free than their masters. The Hunter-Gatherers' collective lack of interest in the loftier ideals means that of all the tribesmen, their minds are the least burdened by them. The moment that supporting these ideals ceases to benefit them, they will simply walk out and find another tribe that sounds more enticing.

The second and most detestable type is the Shaman. They are the keepers of the faith. In contrast to the Hunter-Gatherers, these are the true believers in the tribe's teachings. In their eyes, they have been 'enlightened' to the truth, but this is pure illusion. The most foolish of all notions is the idea that you are nobody's fool. In reality, their brains are mere satellites circling the minds of giants in search of greater meaning. If nothing else, they make good scholars. However, their perceived 'enlightenment' makes them seem like superior intellects (overmen) when they look in the mirror, a class of people better than the world that does not share their exalted values. All who are not 'enlightened' to their way are mindless sheep (untermensch). So, it is their mission to herd the Hunter-Gatherers to their own tribe, thus 'awakening' them to 'the one true path'. Without the first type of tribesman to validate its opinions through sheer numbers, the second type is just another raving fanatic to whom nobody would ordinarily pay any mind. The Shaman always describes itself as a revolutionary. But really, it is only using its so-called 'revolutionary' views as an excuse for offering no true innovations, only romantic commodities. Like any prophet, they will promise you the sun and the moon. Beware, oh brothers and sisters! Beware these 'Promised Land Philosophers', who shall attempt to seduce you with their milk and honey words. Shun them! Drive them from your borders! For they are vampires in disguise and will leech away every drop of your lifeblood if you allow it.

The third and rarest type is the Chieftain. A

superficial glance makes it appear no different from a Shaman. However, closer inspection reveals that this is only camouflage. While the Shamans honestly believe that they are medicine men, the Chieftains recognize that their ointments are snake oil. The keepers of the faith are so cute when they quote legendary brains, which have already done all of the thinking for them, for the purpose of casting the illusion that they too are thoughtful. The Chieftains, the true thinkers, are those whom others quote. The architects of theory. The writers of what all the rest read. No matter what cause, movement, belief or even disbelief the Chieftains may support, they are always Machiavellians first and foremost. Only one romantic commodity can lure them to a tribe; the prospect attaining a position of influence within it! In most cases, this most precious of all prizes is not achieved until years after they are buried in the ground. Future generations then look back upon them in reverence and attempt to live by their teachings. Of all three types, the third is the most likely to be elevated to the status of leader. For while the Hunter-Gatherers and Shamans set out to work for the tribe, the Chieftains set out to make the tribe work for themselves.

Know that there are no 'leaderless' groups. Some may claim to be, but their core concepts and values did not appear magically out of thin air. They were penned by Chieftains, who thus lead by influence if not by direct command. The strength of a leader is necessary for the tribe's existence, for lack of leadership equals lack of direction (which is why no Anarchist movement has ever succeeded in advancing past the grassroots stage). A good leader possesses the qualities of a protector and provider. He shall defend his people with an axe in his right hand and bestow them charity from a bundle of wood in his left. Where I come from, we seek neither a king nor a queen to be leader, but a guardian; one who will protect us from danger and provide for us in times of need. In our eyes, leadership is a burden, not a privilege. We give our rulers the means of sustaining themselves in relative comfort, but they are forbidden from touching any form of currency. Music, stories and recreation for our guardians

are all strictly regulated. Even their spouses must be selected with care. If they have the proper qualities for leadership, they will be able to bear these ordeals. For it takes a true guardian to carry such a heavy burden."

-Translated from Efeu's private journals

She appeared just as she had in Casey's dream.

Resting atop of the mark of the Black Sun was an antique divan with beautifully carved Germanic woodwork and, yes, *real* leather cushions. Sitting comfortably in it was a captivating creature in black. Her milk-white skin was a flash of lightning in the dark. In her elegant claw, she held the tip of a hookah, which would disappear periodically beneath her funeral veil. Its base would then bubble as she took long, intoxicating drags. Yet the smoke which she blew back out smelled neither of nicotine, shisha nor anything illicit. It smelled of almonds, bitter ones at that. The ivory phantasm adjusted herself on the divan and made room for another to sit next to her. She caressed the empty space gently, as if beckoning the boy. Casey felt the predator talons of her superhuman will sink deeper into his soul, pulling him forward.

Join our tribe.

Like a machine, he approached the settee and seated himself beside the *kommandant* of the Thule Society.

"Ekan zich enzuldigam dass minaz Engisken ischt yooaz ne." She said in a soft voice, which contrasted the natural hardness of her language. Casey did not recognize her mother tongue. It reminded him of German, but he had spent enough time in the country to be able to tell that it clearly wasn't German.

Hitler wasn't German either, he reminded himself. *He was from Austria.*

"The *fraulein* apologizes that her English is not very good." Lucy explained.

"Aber, ekan bim ylaoaz dass iuwiz kwemenan." Her mistress continued. *"Furra thinaz untertzung, heutisch motijanan skul wess hant im Englisken. Fallz iuwiz haff ainayas fraggen, leidten am Lucy, zi."*

"But she is happy that you came. For your benefit, today's meeting will be conducted in your native dialect. If you have any questions, you are to direct them to me. Now, Kikka, if you will perform the introductory speech?"

Kikka gave her sister a sour nod. The filthier of the twins stepped in front of the divan. It seemed almost vulgar to have such a dirty person near a being as elegant as her *kommandant*. Casey could see the raw hate in Kikka's eyes as they fixed themselves on him.

It should be me sitting there, he heard her think. He could sense the woman imagining herself in his place, adored by the dark powers and kept safe under the *fraulein*'s wing. He actually found himself feeling sorry for her and wished secretly that there was room on the settee for three. However, all his sympathy was lost the moment that he felt the sharp daggers of resentment stab at him from her brain. He had forgotten that she had a fence of razor wire too. He saw a vision in her mind, a private fantasy of beheading him to prove her superiority. He conjured his own fence quickly, putting a wall between himself and her thoughts. Kikka seemed to wince as the barbed-wire shut her out of his mind. Yet, she managed to compose herself, as well as she could be composed, and adopted the air of an experienced public speaker. Whatever other flaws she might have had, it was obvious that she was quite competent at rousing the rabble.

"Since the beginning of time, history has served as a record of a perpetual conflict between two cosmic forces: Existence and Extinction. Extinction has long sought to consume Existence, which has countered these efforts by rising above and beyond its reach. In the name of self-preservation, Existence created two powers, procreation and evolution. It learned to multiply itself. By adapting to their hostile environments, each generation became stronger than those which came before them. Eight thousand years ago, during the fifth epoch of human development, this process reached its absolute pinnacle. A new race of beings was born from human wombs, overmen with uncanny powers and lifespans of many centuries. On the primitive continent of Hyperborea, these people built a highly advanced civilization. Plato called this kingdom Atlantis. But, in their own ancient Aryan tongue, it was known as Thule. The technology of the overmen became the most advanced of all the realms, inspiring the tales of the Norse gods. But, Extinction would not stand for any of this. Thus, it spawned the Untergeist, the spirit of weakness. This black spectre sowed the seeds of destruction amongst the Aryan overmen. It ruined their health with drugs, smoke and alcohol. It taught them to ignore the value of nutrition in favour of meat and sweets, to live for leisure and find no satisfaction in performing a day of good, hard work. It told them to only admire the greatness of other cultures and to be ashamed of their own heritage. As the centuries passed, their overall value declined. As their strongest became weaker and their smartest became dimmer, Thulean society deteriorated. Finally, when Extinction came in the form of a natural disaster, not one of them possessed the intelligence, skill or physical prowess to prevent it. Thus, the master race and their Fatherland disappeared into the ocean. But although the overmen no longer walk the surface, their legacy lives on in us, the Thule Society. We, the surviving descendants of the Aryan people, have preserved this legacy through the ages."

"Hwat ischt dern ainaz taiknan auz ainaz bat ras?" The veiled figure asked in her own language.

"What is the one mark of a superior race?" Lucy translated.

"The ability to survive." Kikka answered. "For the overman is defined by the act of overcoming."

"Hwat ischt dern streiven furra glikkenstell?" Their mistress said.

"What is the pursuit of equality?" Casey's chauffeur decoded.

"The destruction of greatness." Kikka answered. "It celebrates mediocrity, for one cannot strive to be exceptional without also striving to elevate oneself above their peers. Consequently, one cannot pursue excellence without elitism, advantage and discrimination. As long as anybody possesses something unique, be it a skill or property, the cult of equality shall condemn it as a 'privilege'. In their eyes, we will only be truly equal when everybody has nothing."

"Hwat ischt dern huerste layem auz sors?"

"What is the first rule of magic?"

"That there is no magic. If something appears supernatural, it is because the beholder simply does not understand how it works. The advancement of human knowledge has typically stemmed from attempts to develop rational explanations for seemingly magical phenomena. To accept these phenomena as 'supernatural' is ignorant. To deny their existence is to hinder the advancement of knowledge. So-called 'Nazi mysticism' is merely an effort to reverse engineer ancient wisdom for use in the modern era."

The *fraulein* set her hookah down rose from her seat gracefully. In a strange gesture, she crossed her arms above her head in salute, stretching her claws toward the heavens. There was no doubt in Casey's mind that she would slash the face of Yahweh himself, if she could only reach that high.

"Rahowa!" She shouted. Her congregation of shadows crossed their arms in reply.

"Rahowa!" The living darkness answered.

"Rahowa!" She repeated.

"Rahowa!" The mass called again. They repeated the call over and over, as if singing "hallelujah" from the pews. Even Lucy and Kikka joined in, screaming in a desperate competition of sound.

"Rahowa!"

"Rahowa!"

"Rahowa!"

Casey felt embarrassed that he was the only one not taking part in the reverie. He stood up from the divan and imitated the popular gesture.

"Rahowa!" He cried. *"Rahowa!"*

His voice was lost amongst the collective. A gear in a vast machine. But that was not enough for him. He needed to prove his worth, to demonstrate that Kikka's mistrust was unfounded. He raised his voice above that of the flock and shouted with all his might, dreaming that his cries might drown out all others.

"Rahowa!" He screamed, unaware of what he was screaming. *"Rahowa!"*

Amidst those manic cries, Casey felt like he belonged for the first time.

Join our tribe.

Fight our war.

Share our glory.

At last, the feverish calls ebbed and silence returned to the chamber. The *fraulein* stood regally, as if about to begin a speech. However, she was interrupted by a sudden, cool breeze, which was followed by a low grating. Casey saw the wall swing open and Kitty stumbled forward from the hidden doorway. She walked as though she were in a daze, her pink hair dishevelled, her favourite top ripped, and her black eyeliner streaked with tears. She whispered something in German, but her voice was an indecipherable drone. She shambled towards him like one of the living dead.

A zombie.

Untermensch.

"Hi som alz ob wiz haff lakkjanan ainaz speh." The *fraulein* said.

"It seems as though we have caught a spy." Lucy translated.

Chapter 7

"What is a vampire? It is the most wretched of all creatures on this earth. The Untergeist created it as its ultimate weapon, a human parasite that thrives upon the life energy of others. A being that lives only to take and contributes nothing in return. A healthy mind has the sense to put its tragedies in the past. But the vampire milks tragedy as a resource. It fears responsibility more than anything else and justifies this dread by equating its responsibilities with oppression. It shall paint itself as too meek to carry its own weight, preying upon the sympathies of the well-meaning. Then it shall shoulder its own duties and liabilities onto the rest of the tribe. It pursues self-worth through leisure and recreation and interprets all which hinders this quest as tyrannical. It shall defend itself by seeking pity from altruistic souls, who do not see past the vampire's tears and regard its protection

as a noble, courageous cause. It preaches Slave Morality to the masses. To not give of oneself for the vampire's benefit is, in its eyes, the most shameful of all deeds. But the worst kind are those who boast of their strength, yet never display it. These especially foul creatures always paint the charity that they have received as their own accomplishments, making it appear as though the world is too tyrannical to lend them aid. They claim credit for the accomplishments of others, but never for their own failures. Oh no, if they should underperform, it could never possibly be because they are unskilled. Such a thing would imply personal accountability, which terrifies the vampire. Therefore, it must be that the rest of the world is being unfair and should make special accommodations just for them. It demands that others must pay penance for its own weakness. Thus, the legend of a soulless corpse that feeds upon the blood of the living to prolong its own unnatural existence is a strikingly apt metaphor. As with the myth, the only sure safeguard against such a beast is to drive a stake through its heart."
-Translated from Efeu's private journals

Kitty had no idea what sin she'd committed. All she saw was a haze. She cursed mentally, wondering what had been injected into her veins. She scratched the needle marks on her arm and tried to make sense of her situation. She was in the *Obergruppenführersaal*, but the world around her seemed strange. She was surrounded by those living shadows, like the one that she saw murder that other girl. Had there been another girl? She couldn't be sure. Thinking clearly proved impossible. She had the impression that she had witnessed a murder, but the memory was vague. Her vision was vague too. She must have been seeing double, because when she looked at the blond woman who had taken Casey away from the party, there was a clone standing right next to her. Was she seeing double of Casey too? Probably. There was a figure in black standing beside him. His twin was undefinable in her current state. In fact, all of them were undefinable. When she looked at the crowd of creatures, they had no faces. Only eyes. Each one was just a large, blue eye. Staring at her. Analyzing her. Judging her.

And what was the judge's verdict? The shadows made it clear, even in her fevered state of mind. That living darkness got to work building a makeshift gallows. The noose seemed to come from out of nowhere. Those phantom hands hung it from over the rafters and there it waited, suspended in midair. Waiting to lynch her for her sins.

But what sins? Kitty had no idea. Was it such a crime to be worried about Casey? She had seen him leave the party, seen the sullen look in his heart. She'd watched her red-headed window to the mystical take off in that Mercedes and known that trying to follow it would be a fool's errand. But divining its destination required no stretch of the imagination. It was a simple conclusion that Casey was being taken to the castle, to the place where she had seen the magic reach out and touch him.

The temple of the Black Sun.

She had stuffed some amethyst crystals into her pocket before setting out. She remembered reading online that they could protect her from evil. Well, she saw evil all around her now and she sure needed protecting. So why weren't the crystals working? Why was the evil allowed to triumph?

Admit it, Kitty told herself. *You didn't do this for Casey. You did this because a door had been opened and you wanted to see what was on the other side. Well, now you've seen it. Are you happy with what you've found?*

Her heart pounded so hard that it hurt and the noose still waited. The double-image of the blond lady approached. She seemed split down the middle, as if reflected in a broken mirror. On one side of the glass was a punk, on the other a shrew. A hand which bore a death's head ring dug around in Kitty's pockets until it retrieved her wallet. The double-image read her identification and, funnily enough, the two reflections started talking to each other.

"Katrine Aleksandrov." The shrew said. "She speaks fine German, but has a Russian name."

"A Russian *Jewish* name." The punk added. Kitty felt sick.

"We... we're not religious." She stammered through the haze. She wanted to say more, but the words became a garbled blur in her head. In any case, the twins ignored her cries.

"What do you think?" The punk asked. "Communists?"

"Too young." The shrew replied. "Sending a child to kill and die is more Middle Eastern style."

"Israeli?"

"Precisely."

The snobbish woman fixed Kitty beneath a condescending gaze.

"Look at those brown eyes." She said. "Those low cheekbones. That underdeveloped forehead. She may try to disguise her inferior heritage with that obnoxious hair colour, but she is clearly Jerusalem's daughter."

"Wewelsburg." Kitty responded in her own weak manner. "I-I was b-born in Wewelsburg. Mother was German..."

Tears poured down her cheeks when what she sought to say faded from her drugged mind. Everything was a dream. A nightmare. The only thing she could hope to do was call out and pray that somebody would wake her.

"Casey!" Kitty screamed.

But Casey's eye was vacant. An evil power radiated off of the vague shape next to him. It infected the boy, stripping him of his will.

Stripping him of his soul.

The hellish figure became clearer through the haze. As it did, it giggled like a schoolgirl at her expense. The tip of its hookah disappeared beneath the cloth which covered its face. The creature took a long drag, then blew rings of almond-smelling smoke in the condemned girl's direction. Much to Kitty's surprise, this self-styled *kommandant* spoke to her in German. Granted, it spoke the language in a slow, broken manner, the way one does when they are not terribly familiar with a dialect. But Kitty trembled when she realized that she had heard its voice before.

It was the same voice which had spoken through Casey's lips.

"I warned you." The *fraulein* said. "Didn't I?"

Chapter 8

"What is the purpose of sentience? Why does the human animal, at one end of the evolutionary spectrum, possess an innate understanding of its own individuality while the protozoa, at the other end, lacks even the most rudimentary knowledge of 'self'? While the germ may fight for its survival, it never stops to ask why it must fight. The answer is simply within the development of cognitive functions. Multi-celled life is, by nature, more developed and thus more complex than its one-celled brethren. As the brain becomes more advanced, so does the knowledge of one's own sentience. However, this still does not tell us what role sentience plays. Why must we think of ourselves as individuals? It is quite obvious, is it not? The knowledge of one's own existence, the ability to say 'I am me, I am alive' gives the individual an incentive to preserve its own life. It will then consciously seek ways ways to survive in hostile environments and develop new methods of self-preservation. However, for all these efforts, the individual is still cursed to pass away eventually. At some point, its body shall cease to function and all its efforts to prolong its own existence will prove for nought. What is the purpose of the self-preservation drive if the self cannot be preserved?

Conclusions: *Individuality does not exist for the benefit of the individual. By ensuring their own survival, one ensures the survival of their race. The individual cannot be saved and, for all effective purposes, is already dead. Charity towards it only puts off the inevitable. However, the act of living prolongs the existence of its people. It is akin to a cell in the body. Old cells may die, but new cells will be born to replace them and, thus, the body itself will survive. When the cells actively fight to survive, the body becomes strong. When they put no effort into self-preservation, the body grows weak and vulnerable to sickness.*

What is good? All that strengthens one's own people.

What is evil? All that weakens them."

-Translated from Efeu's private journals

Casey watched as the living darkness set up the gallows. He felt himself tremble when Kitty was finally dragged towards the rope. He could sense her confusion. He could hear her frightened thoughts. To the shadows, her extermination was a policy, not a pleasure. He could sense their feelings as well as hers. They buried their guilt beneath the knowledge that this was their duty. However, Kitty's terror overrode the shadows' cold efficiency. It seeped into Casey's soul, causing his barbed wire to turn brittle with rust. His hard-edged emeralds softened as they fixed the girl under their gaze. He placed a hand on Lucy's shoulder.

"Please." He said softly. His blond Mephistopheles seemed worried by the sympathy in his eyes. He sensed uncertainty race through her mind. Lucy glanced towards her sister, but Kikka only sneered. The words *"I told you so"* appeared in the filthy woman's brain.

"I'm sorry, Casey." Lucy replied. "It must be done."

She gave a heavy sigh.

"Our views are illegal in this country. There are no impartial judges for the likes of us, there are only Ahabs sharpening their harpoons. Would you see me hang in her place?"

Fight our war.

"But... it isn't right." Casey pleaded.

"Ne." The *fraulein* answered. *"Hi ischt rehtaz ne. Hi ischt wranyaz ne augez. Hi ischt nur."*

"No." Lucy translated. "It isn't right. It isn't wrong either. It merely is."

The living darkness looped the noose around Kitty's neck. It would murder her if Casey did not do something. He could feel the claws of that superhuman will lose their grip on his soul.

Fight our war.

They snatched at him and sought to catch him afresh, to wash the empathy from his mind.

Fight our war.

Casey forced his brain free from their clutches. He felt the fence open for Kitty. A special gate was created just for her and his feelings poured through it. He felt his gift reach out towards her in a loving gesture. When it touched her, a purple glow emanated from her pocket. The light pushed the living darkness away from her. Pushed away the hate. Kitty reached into her pocket and retrieved the source of the violet light. A jagged shard of amethyst rested in her palm and bathed the chamber in its incandescence. Casey sensed its power wash over her like a tide of peace. Contentment filled her as the energy surrounded her body, energy that repelled the shadows of the Thule Society as though they were werewolves cringing from silver.

Casey felt his own psionic power magnify. He didn't know how he made it happen, but he brought the executioner's cord to life without even touching it. His gift manipulated the rope, bending it to his will as if it were a serpent. He removed it from around Kitty's throat and compelled it to snake around the ceremonial chamber, blocking off the evil congregation. Now they were on the other side of the fence.

The *fraulein* maintained a cool exterior, although Casey could sense a genocidal rage bubbling beneath those calm waters. Her rage pushed against his fence with a force he had never felt before. Behind that force, he detected a superhuman will.

And an ocean-blue eye.

He tried to beat back the psychic war's tide. Yet for all his efforts, he felt that mental storm flood right through his border. The veiled woman slashed through the rope with her wicked talons and stepped inside his territory. No matter how hard he tried to push her out of his mind, she kept creeping back in.

Join our tribe.

Fight our war.

Share our glory.

"Kwemanan midt mira." She said in a sharp tone. Casey felt drawn to her by something unspeakably powerful. His own blood tugged him towards her.

Join our tribe.

Fight our war.

Share our glory.

"Do not go with her, Casey." Kitty yelled. Her voice snapped him out of his waking sleepwalk. The *fraulein* said nothing, but fixed her attention on the pink-haired girl. Casey never saw any living thing move so fast in his entire life. Before he even knew that she'd budged, the veiled woman had sprinted to the other side of the chamber. Her claws were spread, ready for the kill.

Claws that were strong enough to shred his barrier.

Claws that could rip out Kitty's heart.

Both the attacker and the victim pulled at his loyalties. Tearing him between two conflicting duties. Kitty's eyes widened in horror as the talons threatened to slice through the rainbow-coloured letters on her chest.

"No!" Casey screamed.

And, without any control, he unleashed his gift upon the world.

End of Part I

The Empty Eyes of The Scarecrow

"I first met the Brock family in early 1934, before the war officially started. Alfred Brock was just a slip of a lad at the time and gifted with a bounty of youthful curiosity. During my subsequent visits to the New World, I always made sure to check in on him and his small clan. It was I who taught them the mystic arts and how to use them to ensure a good harvest. As little Alfred grew into a man, he became somewhat enamoured with me. I was flattered, of course, but explained to him how such a coupling was not meant to be. I think the meaning of my words sank in as he grew to an elderly gentleman and I remained a mere maiden. Still, a mutual respect remained and he often sought my expertise on matters which were beyond his mental capacity.

For example, he found himself confused on an issue of what defines us as people, our inner thoughts or our outer deeds? I answered him in favour of the latter, for it is our actions which shape the world, not our ruminations. A million good intentions are not worth as much as a single good act. So too are a thousand intellectual ideas not as valuable as one intelligent deed.

Let this be a warning to all who read these pages. Any society that places a high value on intelligence shall inevitably place a higher value on the mere appearance of intelligence. It will come to praise lofty-sounding but ultimately empty ideas more than intelligent courses of action. However, no thought can substitute a deed. For this reason, I should much rather see a nation of true Herculeses than false Platos."

-Translated from Efeu's private journals

There was no doubt about it, the scarecrow had moved.

Six hours had passed since Sissy and the other pledges had settled into the old Brock farm for the night. Three hours ago, the scarecrow had stood silently in the abandoned cornfield, silhouetted by the bright harvest moonlight. Scarcely one hour ago, it had been a sentinel near the barbed-wire gate. Now, as Sissy looked out the window to the barn, she saw that the protector of the field had disappeared completely. She turned away and paced nervously.

Once, this room had been home to a flock of sheep. Sissy almost suspected that, despite her education, she too was just another member of the herd. She had dreamed of being accepted into Alpha sorority. She wanted to be a sister so badly that she was willing to do any degrading thing that she was asked. At least, she thought that she was. Here it was Hell Night and her final hazing was to spend the night in the old Brock farm's barn. If she could do that, then she would be an Alpha sister. But with each crawling hour, her feet grew colder. After all, they said that old Alfred Brock had been some kind of Neo-Nazi. They said that he had used the Thule Society's secrets to ensure his farm's prosperity. Sure, he was long gone now. But Sissy could not shake the feeling that the magic remained, that this entire decrepit land was somehow alive.

And there was no doubt about it, the scarecrow had moved.

The scarecrow which had worn a swastika armband. Even now, no bird dared to settle in the wild cornfield. But Sissy had dared. She was not a bird. Birds were free. No, she was a sheep spending a night in the barn. But not anymore. To hell with the sorority. To hell with every sorority. Sissy broke from the herd. She stretched her wings and opened the barn door.

And there it stood.

The silent guardian of the cornfield. The scarecrow with the swastika armband. Its empty eyes stared into her soul as it gripped a pitchfork in its gloved hands. Sissy screamed, a scream that was met with laughter.

From either side of the door emerged a respective figure. It took Sissy a moment to recognize them in the moonlight. Emma Lin and Keisha Goldberg, the Alpha sisters who had cooked up this little adventure. They reeked of alcohol as they giggled their heads off at Sissy's expense.

"Real funny, you guys," she said with boiling blood. However, before either of the sorority sisters had a chance to reply, the scarecrow's hollow eyes flashed blood-red and the barn's musty odour was overpowered by the bitter almond smell of Zyklon-B. The silent sentinel plunged its pitchfork into Emma's back. She screamed in terror and agony as the monster twisted its weapon in her young flesh. Then, the screaming stopped and Emma's corpse was tossed aside like a rag doll.

Keisha froze as the scarecrow fixed its eyes on her.

"Please," she pleaded, "I don't wanna duh-duh-die."

She fell to her knees and prayed to the silent sentinel. But this graven image offered no salvation. No forgiveness. No mercy.

The prongs of the pitchfork found her throat. Keisha gagged and choked on her own blood. Her body twitched in death spasms, then became still.

Sissy was the only one left. A stupid lamb who had been led right to the slaughter. It was almost funny how she had once imagined everyone else as being a flock. She supposed that everyone did. Tears streaked down her face when she saw the irony.

"I'm not one of them," she cried, "Please, I was going to leave. I'm..."

She gagged as her eyes fell on the two corpses.

"I'm not a sheep."

The scarecrow stood still. Sissy could feel its red eyes probing her in body and soul. It lowered its weapon and pointed to the door.

"Th-thank you," she said. She raced out as fast as she could into the night air. She alone had been spared from that walking holocaust. As she ran, she heard the death screams of the other pledges. The bleating of sheep in a slaughterhouse.

When the sun rose the next morning, the scarecrow stood silent and still in the abandoned cornfield. It had ensured the farm's prosperity.

The End

<u>Chapter 9</u>

*"Every way of thinking makes the distinction between overman and untermensch, it merely assigns them different labels. The 'overmen' are those who separate themselves as wheat from the chaff, whereas the 'untermensch' are the degenerates whom one must never try to emulate. The Shamans are typically the ones who cast these roles, basing their criteria on allegiance to the tribe. 'Goodness' shall come not from any deed or thought, but by membership to the Shamans' congregations. 'Evil' shall be all that does not conform to their preachings. For example, the common name for 'untermensch' is now 'sheep'. The term is employed to manipulate the audience into feeling that those who do not agree with what the Shaman says have been 'brainwashed' by society. Consequently, it will also create the feeling that in order to be an 'overman' (the word will rarely be used outright, but the idea is still there) who is insusceptible to society's 'brainwashing', one must believe what the Shaman says. In this manner do all tribes make similar estimations of people's worth. To the religious, the sinners are an inferior race. Yet, to the unbelievers, everything non-secular is degenerate. To the Capitalist, poverty makes one an untermensch. To the 'equalizer', advantage is the cause of all inferiority and must be exterminated. As long as anybody can be interpreted as 'advantaged' in even the vaguest of ways, their war for equality will never be over (**Note:** while it is quite true that I would not be as elite as I am had I been spawned from their stock, I can guarantee that none of these 'equalizers' would have been any better off born amongst my kind). The Soviet Union once saw the 'Imperialists' on the other side of the Iron Curtain as subhuman, while these same 'Imperialists' (American Capitalists) saw them in exactly the same manner.*

Even in art, the terms 'highbrow' and 'lowbrow' are references to evolutionary development, subtly implying that superior minds prefer the former while only an inferior mind would prefer the latter. Have you ever seen a Shaman discuss art or literature? They are truly laughable creatures when they do. Lacking even the most basic ability to understand the virtue of creativity, they judge every work solely for how well it mirrors their existing political/social/scientific/spiritual views. For this is their only measure of quality. They label all that shares their rhetoric as exalted, while all that questions it is degenerate.

After all, only a 'sheep' would not be able to see their 'truth'."

-Translated from Efeu's private journals

The death of Adolf Hitler occurred on Walpurgisnacht, 1945.

With Germany defeated, the Allied powers found themselves disagreeing over which of them had earned the right to reap the conqueror's spoils. The end result of these squabbles was that the country was divided into four sectors, all of which converged at Berlin. Each sector was occupied by one of the victorious nations; France, Britain, America and the Soviet Union, respectively. To enforce her rule over the Soviet sector, Russia began constructing a barrier in the capital. In 1961, she started out with a simple barbed-wire fence, then escalated her efforts, culminating them in the erection of the Berlin Wall. The once busy intersection of Potsdamer Platz became a kilometre of no man's land, which one entered at the risk of gunfire. Unbeknownst to the rest of the world, Hitler's bunker lay hidden beneath that forbidden zone. For twenty-eight years, it remained undisturbed while bullets cut through flesh on the streets above it. As if the Fuhrer's ghost was reaching out from underground to claim even more victims, one hundred and thirty six people were murdered by Russian soldiers while attempting to escape from the Soviet sector.

When the Berlin Wall was finally torn down in 1989, it marked the end of Czernobog Aleksandrov's tour of duty. As a soldier of the Soviet Union, he had spent the past five years guarding the border faithfully. Violence never brought him any pleasure. It was just a job. On the day of his discharge, he was sitting in a German coffee shop, wondering what to do with the rest of his life, when the woman of his dreams walked in.

Greta.

He remembered finding it ironic that such a beautiful lady could own such a plain name. They had chitchatted for several hours, discussing everything from the weather to current events and even raised their mugs in honour of the wall's collapse. Although he'd possessed no formal education on the subject, his knowledge of European history must have impressed her. The following day, he woke up to find that he had a job with the German Ministry of Education, Science and Culture. It was all thanks to her. Those were the happiest years in his life, so happy that he could never recall how many they were. The entire period was simply a euphoric daze.

That period ended when Greta became his wife.

They had settled in Wewelsburg with the intention of starting a family. He was not sure when the fights began. It had definitely been after Katrine was born. All he knew for certain was that, after years of courtship, he was no longer good enough for her. Every day, Greta had drifted further from him, until he came home one evening to discover that she had simply left. Thus, the woman of his dreams walked out of his life and didn't even bother bringing their child with her.

Katrine.

She hated that name, preferring to have her friends call her "Kitty" instead. She looked more and more like her mother with each passing day and showed him just as much resentment. Czernobog had done his best to raise the girl on his own. Perhaps he should have been firmer with her. The party downstairs was just one of her many acts of defiance against him. These acts had begun with her hair, as if the lovely auburn locks which she had inherited from Greta were unfit to grow from her scalp. He could not blame the girl for not wanting the same hair as the mother who had walked out on her. However, he did not find it fair of her to blame him for driving the woman away.

She was the one who left us, he thought.

Then came the tantrums, the fights and her buying into all that New Age nonsense. Even when he tried to discipline the girl, she would just ignore his demands, often vanishing from their home for days on end. The man was a stranger in his own house, forced by fate to share his life with a daughter who despised him. He would never dream of walking out on her too, but she needed more guidance than he had the ability to give.

They told me that the wall had been ripped down. Yet I see it now, standing between us.

It broke his heart to think about the time that her club at school had formed a protest group, at their own teacher's behest no less. Academic institutions were meant to prepare youth so that they can function in the adult world. However, he found that the schools were now training children to be nothing more than political activists without any life skills.

Czernobog could not recall what was being protested. If asked, he doubted that any of the protesters would recall it either. Not truthfully at any rate. All he remembered was that, for three days, the five block radius surrounding the Buren *Rathaus* became a warzone. The police clashed with the marching hordes as bricks were thrown, cars were set on fire and slogans were chanted at screeching volumes. He resisted the urge to make any comparisons to the Brownshirts, recognizing Godwin's Law. However,...

If this is how they behave when they have no power, just imagine how they will behave when they do attain it.

There was no doubt in his mind that they would attain it eventually. It was inevitable that this generation would someday spawn a leader after his own had sought retirement. It was quite possible that, in his own lifetime, he would see an entire government populated by cherub-faced children who were born after the Berlin Wall had fallen. He wondered, would such a regime recognize the mistakes of the past or would it merely repeat them?

Only two policies are non-partisan; violence and corruption. Nobody has a monopoly on either.

Katrine's favourite shirt had the word "freedom" printed on the front in bright rainbow letters. Czernobog wondered if she even knew what that word meant.

As he sat in his study, attempting to drown out the din of his daughter's party with a book in his native Russian, he pondered these ideas. He was so engrossed in his thoughts that, at first, the light tap on the door failed to register in his brain. Only after it repeated itself three of four times did he think to answer.

"Yes?" He called in German.

"Herr Aleksandrov?" Said a timid voice on the other side. Czernobog guessed that it was Sarah Lin, the least objectionable of his daughter's many friends.

"There is someone at the door for you." She finished. Czernobog thanked her and wondered who might be foolish enough to come visit him while Katrine was throwing one of her wild bashes. Most likely is would be Mrs Morgan, who had not been in the country long enough to learn how hazardous the Aleksandrov household could be for level-headed adults.

But was Rebecca Morgan as level-headed as she appeared?

Professionally, he had learned to respect the woman. She was quite the architect and she never failed to seek his opinion on how her liberties with the castle's design would affect its historical significance. However, the scene from the previous evening, the look on her son's face as she dragged him from the *Obergruppenführersaal*, haunted him. One may be able to disguise their own volatility with a mask of serenity, but the wounds they leave on others will always give them away. Czernobog had not slept well after witnessing their family drama. He'd lay awake for hours with a worry-filled heart. Was it his place to intervene in their affairs? He had no evidence to take to social services and was uncertain of what would happen to the boy even if he did.

What if I intervened and she faced no consequences? He thought. *What fury would she unleash on him then?*

The smell of drunkenness greeted him as he opened the door to his study. At least it was not marijuana. The excesses of the new generation surrounded him on his path to the front door. They called it a party, but for many, this had become their pursuit in life. It was the Weimar era all over again. The 1920s German lifestyle was making a comeback in a big way and this time it was not limited to any single nation. People everywhere were living like cavemen dancing around a celebratory fire and raising their spears in homage to Bacchus. When this conduct inevitably proved impractical for surviving in the real world, its followers would cry unfairness and blame their failures on something external. They would blame the system. They would blame the rich. They would blame religion. They would blame a race. The only thing that they would never blame was their own bad choices, for such a premise would be unthinkable.

And if some Napoleon were to proclaim "It's not your fault, it's *their* fault", they would believe it blindly.

Rebecca Morgan seemed terribly anxious as she waited for him by the entrance. Czernobog found it jarring to see her in such a state. The raven-haired beauty, normally so professional save for that one slip, was practically in tears. He felt himself softening at the sight of her panic-stricken form. Her crimes, or perhaps they were only perceived crimes, were totally forgotten with one look in her moist, reddening eyes.

"Have you seen Casey?" She asked. Czernobog detected a slight tremble in her voice. He made a quick scan of the teenaged crowd. His eyes were not what they used to be. He had taken to wearing a pair of rimless glasses in recent months. But even with them, the inebriated masses appeared as little more than a blur, obscured by his poor vision.

"He should be around." He replied without certainty. "This is his party."

"No, Casey left." Said a little voice behind him. He had been so wrapped in his own mind that he had not even noticed Sarah Lin follow him from his study. His eyesight must truly be failing him.

Do the thoughtful spend so much time in their own heads that they cannot recognize

"He left?" Mrs Morgan snapped. Her body quivered and beads of sweat formed on her brow as her emotions overtook her. She clasped the girl by the shoulders and shook her. "Why? Where did he go?"

"I-I do not know." Sarah answered. Afraid, she shrank from the older woman and slid free from her commanding grip.

"I... I said some things that I should not have." She explained. "I think he overheard me. Kitty went after him."

Mrs Morgan's eyes widened in fear and rage.

"Was he with anyone when he left?" She asked through gritted teeth.

"*Jah.*" The girl replied. "There was a blond woman... in a suit."

This news came as a blow to the raven-haired architect. Her whole body seemed to sink in depression and defeat.

The discussion was cut short by the delicate jingle of Czernobog's cellphone, which he answered promptly.

"*Da?*"

"P-Papa..." Replied the voice of his daughter. Her tone was the same as when she had called him on the day of the protest.

After the police had picked her up.

When she needed him to rescue her from her own mess.

"What is the matter, Katrine?" He asked her. He never called his daughter by her nickname. "Is Casey with you?"

"I am in trouble, Papa." Katrine whimpered. He could tell that she was crying. "It is Casey. He... he..."

"Calm down." Czernobog said in a steady tone. "Where are you?"

He heard his daughter swallow before replying.

"The castle." She answered.

"Stay where you are." He instructed her. "I will be there shortly."

Czernobog's mind regressed from village historian to cold warrior, from Wewelsburg to Potsdamer Platz. The Imperialist wolves were at the door once more, perhaps they had never left,

and he was on the front line. Only this time, his daughter was the one stranded in no man's land. He had to get her back over the wall before someone opened fire. Maybe this time she would stay on the eastern side, where it was safe.

Maybe this time she would love him.

He was a little unnerved by the ease with which he had switched gears back into his old mode of thought. Perhaps forgotten influences never really die, but lay stewing in the subconscious, colouring our perceptions without our knowledge.

Czernobog put his phone away and turned his attention back to Sarah Lin. He normally regarded her as a bad influence on Katrine, but now he was thankful to have her present. Whatever other faults she may have, she was a loyal friend to his daughter and he knew that he could depend on that loyalty.

"I am going out." He explained to her. "I need you to make sure that everything remains under control here. Understood?"

Sarah gave a nervous nod.

"I may have to call." He continued. "So stay by the telephone."

"Okay." She replied. Czernobog put the hand of authority on her shoulder and looked into her round, eastern face.

"I am counting on you." He told her. He noticed a hint of pride creep into the girl's almond-shaped eyes. That made him feel a bit more comfortable. He let go of her shoulder and headed for the door.

"What happened?" Mrs Morgan demanded. She dogged the man's footsteps, anxious for an answer.

"It seems that our children have gotten themselves in a little trouble." He answered. "Come, I will drive."

He led her to his car and it was not long before they were on the road towards Wewelsburg Castle. The woman was silent for the entire trip. Czernobog wondered what was going through her head, what sort of punishments she might be dreaming up for her son. He had always found it cruel to harm a child. It reminded him of years before. There were two small children at

Potsdamer Platz, twin girls if he remembered correctly. They had raced across that barren kilometre with their family, but only the two of them made it to the wall itself. None of the other guards saw them scale it, that they even could climb over it was one of the great mysteries of the past century. But they must have managed the task somehow, for they had simply vanished from the eastern sector, never to be seen again. Wherever those sisters were, he hoped that they lived prosperously and that they had found it in their hearts to forgive him. No matter how far he travelled, one foot still remained at the Berlin Wall. It had stained him in a way that would never fade. He wondered if this was how war criminals felt. Recalling the incident made him feel dirty and that same dirt always made itself known whenever the time to discipline his daughter arose. However, if he had been stricter with her, perhaps Katrine might be better behaved. He was torn between the need to enforce the rules and the shame he felt at having to be the enforcer. If the girl could only command better control over herself, the entire issue would be resolved. But, like any child, she had not been born with an innate understanding of right and wrong. These were things which he'd had to teach her. Perhaps therein lurked a better purpose for discipline; not as a punishment but as a means of teaching self-discipline.

He pulled the car up at the end of the castle's bridge. He found it curious that a vintage Mercedes was parked not too far away and wondered who else might be visiting the old fortress at such a late hour. Even after he and Mrs Morgan had stepped out of his own Volkswagen Beetle and were trekking across the long, stone platform leading to the entrance, he could not stop glancing back at that antique vehicle. It seemed out of time, but not out of place. The Mercedes-Benz 770 had been a favourite car among the Nazis. However, he decided that he should not read too much significance into its presence. After all, even the Beetle had originally been built as an inexpensive and cheerful buggy for the merry people of the Third Reich.

Volks wagen.

The people's car.

A night watchman greeted the pair at the front door. They were no strangers to the castle's staff and were even expected to drop in at all hours of the night. It simply came with the job. Czernobog was rather relieved to see the man in good spirits, which suggested that he was unaware of whatever hailstorm waited inside. This, in turn, suggested that the other guards did not know about it either and that the authorities had not been contacted. Whatever trouble Katrine had found herself in, its legality was not an issue yet. Which meant that there was still time to deliver her from the jaws of evil. Once inside, he made a guess that his daughter was most likely where she had been the last time he'd found her adventuring after hours. He headed towards the north tower with Rebecca in tow. Sure enough, Katrine was waiting for them by the entrance to the *Obergruppenführersaal.* Tears had streaked through her black mascara and she shivered as if frozen.

What did that boy do to my daughter? He thought, remembering how violence had a way of begetting more violence.

"Where's Casey?" Mrs Morgan demanded in a tone that Czernobog did not appreciate.

"He is in there." Katrine answered, gesturing into the ceremonial chamber. She moved and spoke as if in a trance. Her pupils were dilated. The man wrapped his daughter in a protective embrace, wanting her to know that everything would be okay. He had not held her like that since she was a little girl. While he attended to his child, Mrs Morgan sought her own. She disappeared into the chamber as Czernobog stroked his daughter's pink hair and whispered uncertain assurances in her ears. It was not long before he heard the mother's voice emanating from the next room.

"Casey!" She scolded angrily. "What do you think you're..."

She cut her sentence short and the sudden silence frightened Czernobog.

"A-Aleksandrov..." He heard the woman call with a trembling voice. Czernobog looked into the two earthy fields that his daughter had for eyes and she told him all he needed to know with a simple nod. Reluctantly, he let Katrine go and followed Mrs Morgan into Hitler's ceremonial chamber.

In the darkness before him stood an enormous spiderweb. He had thought it impossible for any eight-legged creature to spin a snare so monstrous. A poor fly had even been caught in its gigantic mesh. A young, blond lady in a smart business suit was trapped, tangled in the webbing. She struggled in vain to free herself. Only once his weak eyes adjusted to the dim light did Czernobog see that the web was but a simple rope tied to each of the surrounding pillars, creating a fence-like wall of cord. Behind that wall, curled in a foetal position, was a pale, shivering shape of a boy. Casey was barely recognizable as he lay atop the mark of the Black Sun. He was bathed in a cold sweat, his eyes bloodshot with terror. Scattered around him were the splintered remains of a once beautiful, antique divan.

The former soldier almost tripped over an elegant hookah, which sat cracked upon the marble floor, as he took a step towards the fence. His approach triggered a reaction from the thickly bound twine. As if alive, the ropes tautened and tensed, like the coils of a snake, clenching the boy in a constrictor's embrace.

Or like a guard firing a warning shot from above the wall.

Although he had never been religious, Czernobog whispered a Russian prayer. The blond woman winced in pain as her bonds grew tighter. He noticed a silver death's head ring on her left hand, a reproduction of the SS honour rings which were awarded to the Nazi elite. It was decent enough quality, but not the sort that any serious collector would spent their money on. However, such items were regarded as illegal contraband in Germany. The situation was growing more dire by the second.

Which meant that Katrine's situation was dire.

From above his head came a soft creak. Although it was faint, it came as a gunshot to his ears. He convinced himself that it was just the building settling, but felt compelled to look

upwards all the same. Mrs Morgan must have heard it too, for she followed his gaze to the overhanging darkness.

Czernobog's eyes were not what they used to be. At first, he could only make out a sort of blurry pendulum swinging overhead. But then his vision began to clear and a he trembled at what came into focus.

He began reciting another prayer, one that his mother had taught him in secret.

One in Hebrew.

What have you done, boy?

The chamber's rafters were a gallows for a woman in a long, black dress. With a noose around her broken neck, she swayed limply from right to left while the rope which hanged her creaked from the strain. Her face was hidden beneath a funeral veil. But, at one angle, Czernobog's normally poor eyes received a brief but very clear view of what lay under it.

And he froze in horror at the sight.

"What in God's name is that thing?" He muttered out loud without even meaning to.

"I don't know." Mrs Morgan lied.

Chapter 10

"Propaganda is a necessary tool of any tribe. The term is derived from an administrative wing in the Catholic Church which was formed in 1622, the 'Congratio de Propaganda Fide' or 'Congregation for Propagating the Faith'. Its role within its own tribe was the spreading of Catholic ideas to Non-Catholic countries. Thus, the word 'propaganda' refers to any media, including literature, visual arts, dramatic performances, memes, broadcasts, music, editorials and even the spoken word, which attempts to propagate an idea. However, in the past century, humanity has developed negative associations with the word 'propaganda'. As a result, individual tribes have now taken to using it exclusively as a condemnation of any message which contradicts their own.

For example, in my Fatherland, the most popular stories are dramas about the vices of crime and corruption. It does not matter that their authors have never seen so much as a petty theft, they are never called out as 'propagandists'. Culturally, we champion these tales for their 'insightful' portrayals of the subject matter, despite the fact that they were conjured wholly out of cloth and offer no true insights at all. What they do instead is proliferate a popular narrative and, thus, propagate its ideas. The themes being represented are not particularly intelligent either, but we have labelled them as 'intelligent' when they conform to a certain rhetoric. In so doing, we spread the social narrative that this type of story, with this type of message, is simply what appeals to intelligent people. We may then feel that we too are intelligent for consuming these stories in bulk and that those who prefer other kinds possess intellects which are inferior to our own. With this prejudice firmly in place, we can enjoy the illusion of an intellectual discourse without any risk of having our views contradicted or challenged. Only if the work in question does not conform to this rhetoric do we then condemn it as 'propaganda'.

If one thing is certain about propaganda, it is that vice sells, particularly when it is projected upon the enemy. Humanity tends to think in very black and white terms. If one side in an argument is wrong, it is typical, perhaps even instinctive, to assume that the other side is right. The antithesis of the romantic commodity is the ad hominem attack. Rather than increasing the perceived value of one's own tribe, it decreases that of its competitors. When one lacks a legitimate rebuttal to the enemy's argument, they simply gloss it over and attack the enemy's character instead. Amongst the Shamans, this is referred to as a 'strawman argument', at least when another directs it towards them. Concepts such as 'cruelty', 'sadism', 'oppressiveness', 'ineptitude', 'incompetence', 'hate' (and 'hate speech' consequently), 'sin', 'immorality', 'sexual deviancy', 'psychopathy', 'sexism', 'racism' and, yes, even 'Fascism' and 'Nazism' are usually employed for the sake of evoking negative emotions in the listener, making it seem as though the target of these accusations is a monster whose views should be ignored outright. In this manner, one side in a conflict appears 'good' by sheer virtue of the opposing force being 'bad'. What is the most common of all ad hominems? By far, it would have to be 'evil'. Take, for example, a poster that the Propagandaministerium published during the war, one which depicted an innocent German girl being violated by Russian soldiers. This piece proved so effective at convincing the public of their adversary's evil nature that, whenever the Soviets conquered a German village, many women would prefer to commit mass suicide rather than face their 'liberators'."

-Translated from Efeu's private journals

The ropes around Lucy's wrists and waist dug into her skin, but they did not cut her nearly as much as the sight of the man's face. It was already embedded deeply into her memory, haunting her nightmares and poisoning her every waking moment. She had expected to never see him again and yet he stood before her now. Perhaps it had been a part of her mistress's plan that this reunion should occur. After all, who could fathom what had gone on inside of that woman's superhuman brain? He was older than she remembered and had taken to wearing glasses, but there was no mistaking him. Mrs Morgan had called him "Aleksandrov". That snotty Jewish girl had called him "Papa". Lucy had to admit that she was taken aback to discover that the man was a father, but she supposed that it really should not come as a shock. Comparing his features to his daughter's, she could see the Untergeist lurking in both of their faces. Had her hands been free, she would have strangled the old man in an instant, erasing him all his kin from the face of the earth.

Lucy and Kikka had been but children when they'd raced across Potsdamer Platz with lead shells chasing after them. Their family was fleeing the Soviet Union, fleeing the KGB, to the land of plenty which was promised to lie on the other side of the Berlin Wall.

But none of them ever made it to the west.

She had a vivid recollection of the border guards' faces as they took aim, especially the one who was targeting the back of her mother's head. He had seemed so cold. So terrifying. Then came the loud cracks of ballistic fire. The people's guns fired bullets of equality and freedom, liberating her family from the oppression of this mortal coil. Lucy and Kikka hid amongst the rubble for hours, expecting a patrol to come and execute them at any second, until a miracle occurred. The ground underneath them gave way and the sisters fell together, down the rabbit hole, into a subterranean cavern which had remained secret for years.

Hitler's bunker.

It was there that the *fraulein* found them. She had stayed in that underground fortress since the end of the war, using her psionic powers to play both sides of the wall for fools. There, she had waited with impossible patience for her time to come again. She hated the Soviets just as much as the twins did. Hated them for their betrayal. She took the girls under her wing and fixed their little rabbit hole before the guards had a chance to discover it. She sheltered them in that lost bastion. She fed them preserved food which had been meant for a Fuhrer. She protected them faithfully and told them bedtime stories about her Fatherland and the Reich's glory days. Instead of Marx, Engels and Trotsky, Lucy's reading list now consisted of Nietzsche, Machiavelli, *Mein Kampf* and *Zweites Buch*. The girls also read about Doctor Mengele's experiments at Auschwitz and how he had believed that the answer to breeding a superior race lay within twins. His theory was that the features which they had in common were those that they had inherited from their Aryan background, while differentiating features were created by degenerating environmental factors. It filled Lucy with pride to note that, aside from their personal tastes in clothes and hairstyles, she and her sister were indistinguishable from each other.

According to Doctor Mengele, they were the master race.

Instead of worshipping the great lie called "Equality", she now sought to elevate herself. She strove to be as intelligent and as physically fit as she could, so that she might be deserving of such a majestic title as "superior". As far as she was concerned, Hitler's only crime was being born before his time. She was not blind to the rising sense of nihilism that was permeating western culture and the collapse of conventional ideals which accompanied it. Nietzsche had called this phenomenon 'the death of God', the decay of traditional Judaic and Christian morals. Weimar era Germany in the 1920s had not been very different from the modern world. Following the Great War, the Fatherland was left a desolate place, its people disillusioned, impoverished and destitute. Then, just as Nietzsche had prophesied, an overman came to usher new morals and create a new civilization. His methods might have seemed cruel, but whenever one builds from the ashes of a corrupt society, harsh and even violent means always prove necessary to maintain order. It was for this same reason that Vlad the Impaler was hailed as a hero in his native Romania, even though the rest of the world saw him as a bloodthirsty monster who inspired the legend of Dracula. He was an overman too.

However, although God was certainly a dead ideal in Weimar Germany, he was alive and well everywhere else on earth. The morals that he represented mobilized the League of Nations against Hitler and it took nearly every one of them to defeat him.

What does that one, final failure matter anyways? When Plato attempted to apply his theories in Syracuse, he made an even bigger clown of himself. Yet, that has never prevented either Democrats or Republicans from romanticizing the old Mediterranean.

Sadly, the world had not yet been ready for the overman. He had come, but humanity proved unworthy of him. Now, however, Lucy sensed the Untergeist, the spirit of nihilism, the spirit of *weakness*, casting its shadow over a greater part of the world. The 'death of God' had finally run its course. Like Atlantis sinking into the ocean, Babylon crumbling to the desert sands or Rome being picked apart by the Barbarian Invasions, the old institutions were dying a slow but certain death. The time was finally ripe for the rise of her tribe. If Germany invaded Poland today, she wondered if England would still feel duty bound to liberate the oppressed people. Or, would the English merely shrug their shoulders and proclaim that it is not their business to interfere with the affairs of other nations?

The man called "Aleksandrov", the man who killed Lucy's mother, approached the web of hangman's rope. He stood before the little girl that had escaped him all those years ago and looked at her as if through a rifle's scope.

"Who are you?" He asked.

Don't you recognize me? She thought. She supposed that he must have so much blood on his hands that the faces of all his victims simply blurred together. Her family was nothing but notches on his gun.

"We are the Thule Society." Lucy answered.

"*Niet*, you are not." Aleksandrov continued. "The real Thule Society was shut down in the twenties after most of its prominent members left and joined the Nazi Party."

She raised an eyebrow, impressed with his historical knowledge.

His wealthy parents probably paid to get him the best education, she thought. *They have all the money. They can buy anything.*

"You might have heard the claims that they formed an occult circle within the SS?" She said. "A group of their twelve most elite, philosophical minds?"

"*Da.*" He answered. "But nothing has ever been substantiated."

A mocking smile crossed Lucy's face.

"Consider them substantiated now." She said. The man remained unmoved.

Still so cold...

"Alright." He said. "Tell me, then, what is that... that..."

He cast his sniper's eyes upwards, towards the angel hanging from heaven. Lucy's guardian dangled lifelessly from the ceiling, as if the Nuremberg trials had finally caught up with her.

"... that... *thing.*"

Mrs Morgan had remained silent for the entire conversation. However, Lucy knew that there was nothing suspicious about her behaviour at all.

"Are you going to tell him or shall I?" She called to the dark-haired woman. Casey's mother shrank like a scolded child. Even she bore the

features of an inferior race, features which she had passed on to her son. But the *fraulein* had assured the twins that he was not tainted by her genes. Kikka never believed it, but Lucy felt certain that her guardian angel knew what was for the best. After all, she had been an authority on these matters.

"Don't believe a word that woman says." Lucy told Aleksandrov. "She knows perfectly well what's going on here. She's known for years and has dreaded the coming of this day."

The blond woman paused for a second to collect her thoughts. She had read so much literature, sifted through so much scripture, that organizing the ideas in her head often proved to be a chore.

"Have you ever heard of Hitler's search for Atlantis?" She said at last.

"*Da.*" Aleksandrov answered. "He believed it was the birthplace of the ancient Aryan race. The Nazis spent more money trying to find it than the Americans spent on developing the atomic bomb."

Lucy did not appreciate his tone.

"Yes." She continued. "Some theories put it at the north pole, others in Greenland, others still in the Canary Islands. There was a Doctor Baldur Wolf whose ideas became very popular in Berlin. In 1938, he led an expedition to find the sunken kingdom. No one knows where he went in that time. All we know is that, when he came back, he had that woman with him."

Lucy's sapphire eyes widened to fanatical proportions.

"Casey is Doctor Wolf's grandson."

Aleksandrov snorted.

"Even if there was any plausibility in what you are saying, that boy looks a little young to be the grandchild of a Nazi war criminal." He scoffed. Mrs Morgan approached him with a sullen gait, her dark eyes cast downwards in shame. Something was on the tip of her tongue, something she wished not to speak.

"When I met his father, he was already more than twice my age." She explained. "But he didn't look a day older than me. If anything, he looked younger."

"How is that even possible?" The sniper-eyed man asked.

"Go on and tell him." Lucy chided cruelly. "Tell him why that boy can read people's minds. Tell him why your son is so important to the Thule Society. Doctor Wolf is his grandfather, there's no doubt about that. Go on and tell him about his *grandmother*."

Mrs Morgan held her tongue, but cast her gaze upwards, towards Lucy's guardian angel. The significance of the gesture was not lost on Aleksandrov, whose brow furrowed in disbelief.

"You are saying that Casey is..."

"The modern day product of the Third Reich's eugenic experiments." Lucy explained. "Selective breeding for the purpose of engineering a master race was the pillar on which the SS was built. That boy's father was grown in a test tube, with sperm from a Nazi officer and an egg from an Atlantean overman. He was then sent out into the world to spread his seed amongst mortal women, so that they might give birth to a generation of superhumans. If we had won the war, Casey would now be worshipped as a living god. But instead, he is beaten into submission for not being one of you."

Out of the corner of her eye, Lucy spied Katrine creeping around the entrance. She sneered with contempt at the snot-nosed little punk. Everything about her made Lucy feel the need to take a scalding hot shower. Especially that hypocritical slogan on the front of her top.

Freedom.

You see yourself as such a 'rebelle', don't you? She thought. *You think that your obnoxious hair and loud t-shirt make a statement. Do you really believe for a moment that your obscenities offend me? That your hair and clothes shock me? Ha! They only reflect your own immaturity. A truly tyrannical society wouldn't put up with your childish antics for two seconds. Tell me, who makes your hair dye? Where did that shirt come from? Who mixed the pigments, grew the cotton, patented that design, marketed it, mass produced it and sold it in stores around the globe? It certainly wasn't Guy Fawkes. In the end, it is just a product. The slogan it displays is only a logo intended to appeal to your tastes as a consumer, nothing more. You are not a revolutionary, merely another demographic. In fact, by spending money on that top, you have provided financial support to the very establishment that you imagine you're rebelling against. But that didn't stop you, did it? No, you went ahead and bought it anyways, just because it had the word 'freedom' printed on it.*

The foul little beast stumbled towards the web, her drug-addled mind attempting to form a question.

"What about the shadows?" Katrine asked. Her father raised a curious eyebrow.

"Shadows?" He said. "What shadows?"

"Call them whatever you like." Lucy answered. "Ghosts. Phantoms. The shades of bygone wars. You might have noticed that there are twelve of them. The *fraulein* once tried explaining how she brought the original Thule Society back from the dead, but I could never wrap my head around her people's technology. It's beyond anything that we're even close to grasping. However, the vikings used to believe in spirits called the *Einherjar*, the souls of their greatest warriors whom the Valkyries had raptured to Valhalla. Legend tells that they would return to fight the final battle at the end of times. I think that's a very apt description, don't you?"

The captive woman tossed her head back and laughed at the fate she knew awaited this party of *untermenschen*. None of them had the slightest inkling as to what the *Einherjar* had been gathered for. None of them even suspected the extent of Atlantean science, which was so advanced that it looked like magic to humanity's primitive eyes.

But they would all learn soon.

They would all pay.

The girl backed away from her and Lucy saw fear in those rebellious eyes.

"What are we going to do?" Mrs Morgan asked.

"Do what you wish." Aleksandrov replied. "I am going to call the police."

He fished his cellphone out of his pocket and began to dial.

"You can't." The dark-haired woman snapped. For a moment, there was murder in her eyes. However, the moment passed and her rage was replaced with feigned sorrow as she cast her gaze towards the hanging creature.

"Do you have any idea how much trouble Casey will be in if this gets out?" She said in a controlled tone. "He's just a boy, for Christ's sake. Something like this will ruin his life."

"Are you really worried for him?" Aleksandrov said. "Or for yourself?"

Mrs Morgan's eyes became cold daggers.

"What's that supposed to mean?" She demanded, although everyone in the chamber knew the answer. The man did not reply with words, but by meeting her daggers with his own rifle sights.

"May I have one, small request first?" Lucy interrupted. The others were silent as they turned their eyes upon her.

"May I pray?"

There was a still pause in the air.

"I suppose it couldn't hurt." Mrs Morgan said at last. The man nodded and put his phone away.

"*Danke.*" Lucy thanked them both. She closed her eyes and sought that special, spiritual place within herself. It was higher plane of existence. There, she could be one with Mother Nature. Humanity's rules of 'right' and 'wrong' ceased to apply. She was beyond good and evil. In that place, cut off from the outside world, she became a living paradox, brimming with limitless potential as an individual and yet utterly insignificant in the cosmic scheme. She recited an old Icelandic rune prayer, one that she had learned in the bunker.

"Týr er einhendr áss
ok ulfs leifar
ok hofa hilmir.
Mars tiggi."

She cast her eyes upwards, to the one who had taught her to pray like this. Her Aryan Antichrist.

"Rahowa."

A low hum reached Lucy's ears. The Atlantean technology fitted throughout the castle began reacting to the hymn of Tyr in the same manner that a computer reacts to a command code. The chamber was filled by the scent of almonds and in the spot where Casey lay shivering, the mark of the Black Sun glowed as blue as the bottomless sea. The light attracted the others as though they were moths. They stood outside the fence and stared mesmerized by the gleam. It bathed the boy in its splendour, washing the filth from his mind and body, cleansing him of impurity while the twelve shadows swam in the air around him. When the light finally faded, the phantom shapes disappeared and the strange hum ceased. However, Casey looked paler, his eyes redder, and the stench of bitter almonds still hung in the atmosphere.

"You're finally claiming your birthright." Lucy said. *"Alles gute zum geburtstag."*

Curiously, the smell grew stronger, more acrid. Without warning, the *fraulein*'s funeral veil landed on the floor next to Mrs Morgan. Lucy grinned, knowing what its fall from above meant. Everybody but her cast their eyes up to the chamber's ceiling. She did not need to follow their gaze.

She already knew that the noose was now empty.

The *Einherjar* were not the only ones who could be brought back from the dead.

Lucy heard a soft grating sound. It told her that in the short time it took for these *untermenschen* to strain their necks upwards, her mistress had already reached one of the castle's many secret passages. She turned her head just in time to see a large panel on the wall begin to close.

"Do not let it shut!" Aleksandrov shouted. "We cannot let that creature get away!"

He raced across the room in a desperate gamble. For an instant, Lucy thought that his weak human legs would not make it in time. However, he managed to sprint much quicker than she had expected and grabbed hold of the secret door seconds before it could close completely.

"Help me." He called to the others. "I cannot open this by myself."

Katrine rushed to his aid with Mrs Morgan following close behind. They both took hold of the door and pulled with their combined might. Lucy observed with amusement how, for all their culture's boasts about 'independence', it was by putting their individuality aside and operating as a team that their efforts bore fruit. By moving as one, thinking as one and focusing their efforts on a common goal, they found the strength to pry the door open one inch at a time. They were totally dependant upon each other. As soon as the opening was wide enough for someone to fit through, the man peered ahead into the unexplored with the hope of making sure that it was safe to venture further.

And that proved to be his undoing.

Long, black talons reached out from the abyss. They hooked into Aleksandrov's chest and pulled him screaming into the darkness. The door was slammed shut behind him by a superhuman force, but not before Lucy saw a pair of hate-filled beads, as red as Aryan blood, staring out from the unknown. The obnoxious little vampire pounded her fists against the sealed passageway as her father's cries echoed through the ceremonial chamber.

Abruptly, his screaming stopped.

"Papa?" Katrine whimpered. She beat against the wall and called out in sorrowful panic.

But her father did not reply.

Lucy's prayer had been answered.

<u>Chapter 11</u>

"I curse the names of Orwell and Huxley. For many centuries, human behaviour was governed by the Afterlife myth. The people adhered to their tribal laws because they believed that they would be rewarded in the hereafter if they did so. Consequently, they also believed that disobeying these teachings would condemn them to eternal suffering. However, at a certain point in our development, my people learned to doubt this superstition and recognized its influence, thus taking the first step towards progressing beyond it. However, in the surface world, the ashes of the Afterlife myth were not even cold when those two Englishmen repackaged it for the age of materialism. Its form is now political instead of metaphysical, for the political is merely superstition for the secular. As a result, salvation and damnation are now Orwellian legacies for the entire collective rather than spiritual rewards for the individual. Heaven is no longer Disneyland for the dead, but an earthly utopia that one helps to build by following the tribe's doctrines. Instead of Dante's Inferno, Perdition is now a hypothetical dystopia, which is enabled by the act of non-conformity (thus, the fear of subjugation is, quite ironically, used as a tool for enforcing subjugation). 'Oligarchical collectivism' indeed! Show me a single philosophy that has not, in practice, proven both oligarchical and collectivist. But I digress...

If dystopia is the new Hell, who is the Devil? It is certainly not Lucifer, who retired from that position long ago and sought greener pastures as a symbol of youthful rebellion against a theological establishment. Satan is no longer the Prince of Darkness, but the cool kid in class. His cultural successor is, of all things, a painter named Adolf. The Fuhrer has become a sort of bogeyman. An anti-ideal whom one seeks to contrast oneself against and whose name is invoked for the specific purpose of exploiting a common fear. The fear of oppression. The fear of dystopia. In truth, however, there are no dystopias. Nor are there any utopias. There are only societies, any one of which may be described as either free or tyrannical depending on what criteria the individual uses to measure their personal liberty. Thus, whether one lives in Paradise, Perdition or something in between is entirely a matter of their own point of view."
-Translated from Efeu's private journals

Deep below the northernmost tower of Wewelsburg Castle lay the vault. It had been intended to serve as a crypt for the twelve highest ranking officers in the SS. A revered final resting place for Hitler's elite. However, the room remains unfinished to this day.

There they stood forgotten and abandoned, a dozen pedestals arranged in a circle underneath a large, domed ceiling. According to legend, these crumbling altars would have housed the ashes of the Black Sun's knights, so that future generations might worship them as heroes. They surrounded a shallow, marble pit, at the centre of which lay the opening of a rusted pipe. Had the Nazis won the war, this would have served as an eternal flame, whose warmth and light representing the ongoing glory of the thousand year Reich.

Sitting next to this stone cold relic of unrealized ambitions was one of its modern shamans. Kikka had expected to feel smug about being proven right. Instead, she found herself solemn.

We never should have let that boy in, she thought.

The Thule Society had been her and Lucy's private club ever since the day that the *fraulein* found them hungry and frightened in the bunker. She had always known that allowing the boy to join would be a mistake. He was an outsider.

Untermensch.

Subhuman.

There should have been no place for him within their ranks. Yet, Kikka's guardian thought differently. She could never fathom that woman's Machiavellian agendas. They were always kept strictly to herself. Perhaps it was because Casey was her grandson. Even the xenophobic heart of an Atlantean must soften to the subtle chords of parental love's tune. Whatever her reasons, the mistress had been insistent on adding the boy to their little family and that the twins should treat him as a brother.

Try as she might, Kikka never had the strength to refuse her guardian's will. The emblem on her shirt was a constant reminder of the thrall which possessed her.

Totenkopf.

The death's head.

It was strange to think that such a frightening symbol actually represented chivalry. It signified how its bearers were more than willing to lay down their own lives to defend what they saw as a higher cause. Yet, whenever her mistress had exercised that *ubermenschen* will, Kikka had sensed another meaning.

A mark of ownership.

You are nothing, it seemed to say. *Your life has worth solely in its duty to me.*

Even after death, her guardian's voice seemed to speak to her through that printed design.

I own you.

Kikka wondered what her duty to her slain mistress might be. To carry on her mission? Yes, that had to be it. She would not wallow any further. Pity was for the weak, self-pity for the weakest. She had to rescue her captive sister and take blood vengeance upon he who had dared to intrude upon their space.

On he who had presumed to be her brother.

Kikka stood up, tall and proud, and called out to the living darkness.

"Come to me." She commanded. "Efeu is dead. I am her successor. Come to me, oh shades of the Thule Society, and I shall lead you all to the thousand year Reich which Hitler once promised you."

The twelve pedestals stood undisturbed, their shadows unresponsive.

"Come to me." She shouted. "I command you."

Still, the darkness would not obey her. She screamed at the altars and stomped her feet in rage.

And her orders still went without appeasement.

Kikka's fit was disturbed by the scent of bitter almonds. It wafted through the burial chamber, as if someone were pumping it full of deadly Zyklon-B gas. A soft voice reached her ears, humming an operatic chord which sounded vaguely like a nursery rhyme. The vault's unique acoustics amplified the sound, making it seem to emanate from beyond the grave. Her eyes followed it upwards, towards a decorative swastika called the *hakenkreutz*, which adorned the highest point on the ceiling. Slowly, the mark began to turn clockwise, as if unscrewing itself from the planchement. By the miracle of Atlantean technology, it lowered itself from above, a marble platform suspended in the air by beams of blue light.

Kikka stared in disbelief at the ghost who descended atop the marvellous device. Of course, this was not the first time she had seen *fraulein* Efeu survive the impossible. However, regardless of whether the Atlanteans really were immortal or their medicine was merely so advanced that it looked like necromancy to human eyes, the phenomenon never ceased to astound her. That mysterious woman could be torn asunder or dissolved completely in acid. But no matter how much the world sought to burn or bury her, she always just seemed to resurface later on, as if the Hydra were regrowing one of its heads. And each time she returned from the grave, a part of the ocean seemed to return with her. Even now, after being hanged for her atrocities, gills had visibly formed on her face and neck. A greenish tint had crept into her once flawlessly white skin and there, on her ankles, were those fins? Her ruby eyes, marred by the dark rings of an insomniac, glared like daggers from her close-shaven skull.

Efeu smiled at her ward's surprised gaze. She goosestepped off of her platform, which raised itself once more and returned to its proper place in the ceiling.

"Iuwiz yabchen bi-haissiz, Kikka?" She said in her own tongue, which she called "Runespeak". *"Taljanan zi mira dass ischt ainaz schter gaggen."*

Kikka's astonishment gave way to irritation. She might not have been as proficient a translator as her sister, but she still understood what her guardian had just said.

"You giving commands, Kikka? Tell me this is a bad joke."

"Why not?" She said. "Why shouldn't they listen to me? What is so special about you that you can give them commands and I can't?"

"Vielleicht iuwiz habhjanan zi aznojanan ihre raspt ne."

"Perhaps you have not earned their respect."

Efeu's crimson eyes studied Kikka's clothes and hair. She seemed to be regarding an infant who refused to become an adult. Under that gaze, Kikka felt as though she had lived her whole life in Neverland.

I'll show her, she thought.

"You and your people are dinosaurs." She snapped. "It's time for change. I won't make the same mistakes as you. You are the past, I am the future."

Efeu sighed. She closed her bloody beads and a wave of psychic energy washed out from her. Her superhuman will was like a black hole. It pulled all life towards it and drained the universe of any light or hope.

I own you, her mind seemed to say. *You are my knight. You will ally yourself with me unconditionally, you will trust my word absolutely and if I am threatened, you will martyr yourself to protect me.*

Kikka resisted the power of her guardian's mind with every bit of strength she possessed. Her death's head shirt began whispering to her.

Join our tribe.

Fight our war.

Share our glory.

No, she thought. *I shall not bend. Not this time.*

Her resistance was met by a storm of psionic wrath. Refusal to surrender to persuasion was met with forceful repercussions. On the place the Hindu's call the "Ajna", Efeu's forehead opened like a chrysalis and revealed a third eye. That eye was as blue as the eternal ocean and also as deep. An omnipotent force radiated from it, calling the darkness to her. From each of the twelve pedestals, the shadows of the Thule Society came to their mistress's aid. The living darkness covered the walls and stood awaiting her orders.

"Thinaz haut ware skaunitz lamskar makojanan."

"Your skin would make beautiful lampshades."

"Hort diese barnanrei sofort aiththau ikan habhjanan hi von thinaz skreien kark gelt."

"Cease this childishness immediately or I shall have it peeled from your screaming carcass."

Kikka stared into that eye. She sensed her life force drain from within her. Her will to resist decayed into nothing. At last, she lowered her own eyes in submission and felt thoroughly disgusted with herself.

"You are so cruel." She whimpered. Efeu closed her third eye and lit herself a cigarette.

"Hi ischt sade ne."

"It is not cruelty."

"'Sade' ischt di lust in lid dern antherazen."

"'Cruelty' is taking pleasure in the suffering

of others."

"'Harouse' ischt taljanan di barnan, egal vie mekilaz zi woln, habjanan zi nug."

"'Hardness' is telling children that no matter how much more they want, they have had enough."

"Di tatzak dass iuwiz kunanan teln toris ne skauwojanan dass iuwiz ungeignet furra ainaz bihaissiz rankaz sind."

"The fact that you cannot see the difference shows that you are unfit for a position of command."

"Standt?"

"Understood?"

"Yes." Kikka answered.

"'Yes' *hwat?"* Her guardian demanded. The defeated woman lowered her head in resentment.

"Yes, my *kommandant.*"

Efeu's black-painted lips spread into a satisfied smile. She called out to the shadows in Runespeak and beckoned them closer. Teasing them. Seducing them. Kikka watched as her guardian whispered her desires in their ears, a scorpion asking the frogs to carry her across the river. Whatever venom she promised them remained their secret, for Kikka was unable to understand what was being said. However, the *Einherjar* soon approached her and explained their duty.

"We have a situation to contain." One of them said in German. "First, a patrol shall be set up outside of the castle. Nobody comes in or out. Second, our guests upstairs will be watched closely. The *fraulein* desires updates on their status every ten minutes and an immediate report the moment that they start to move. As for you, Kikka, you are to dress in uniform 4-A and feed false information to the staff at the youth hostel. Tell them that there was a shooting and that everybody must stay inside until the situation is resolved. Understood?"

"Jawohl." She replied. The darkness scrutinized her, uncertain of her faithfulness. Or her reliability.

I'll show them, she thought. She stood up straight, at martial attention, and saluted the living abyss.

"Rahowa!" She shouted with strength and conviction. Even Efeu raised a shaved eyebrow in interest.

I'll show them, Kikka thought. *I'll show them that I'm worthy of their respect. I'll show them that I'm better than her... better than that boy.*

The shadows of the Thule Society mobilized with Kikka by their side and paraded through the gated door.

I'll show them all, she thought as her lead-filled boots stomped against the floor. *They'll see.*

***

Efeu watched as her soldiers marched off to wage war with the outside. Her own work in the SS crypt was not yet done. She sat cross-legged and placed her palms on her knees in a meditative posture. She closed her ruby eyes and took slow, deep breaths, easing herself into a tranquil state of mind. Beneath her, the hollow earth spun in one direction while the heavens turned in the opposite over her head. They were like two overlapping swastikas with her centre as their axis. Her third eye, the one which could see beyond the veil, opened once more and she saw the vault as it truly was. It was not a mausoleum. It was a temple. The pedestals were chantries for paying homage to the Thule Society's lost gods. Before her, the pit housed an eternal flame called Hate. It glowed no dimmer nor brighter than it ever had in history. Yet, it still could not be seen without the overmen's special sight. It is always invisible in the present day and only ever reveals itself upon reflection. Those who kept its embers stoked had merely changed their uniforms. Efeu called out to the fire in Runespeak.

For they shared the same tongue.

"Number Eighteen calling General Vrilla." She said. "Eighteen calling Vrilla. Come in, General."

The flame answered her call by rising into a blueish pillar of burning death. Gazing into it, she saw the beautiful horizons of her Fatherland. The sight of the vast, utopian cities and expertly crafted architecture pulled at her heartstrings. Efeu had never taken a spouse. She was married to the

Atlantean state. Every living thing within the sunken kingdom was her husband, for whom the protection and provision were her sworn duties, regardless of the costs. She was their sword and shield upon the surface world. Their agent in the realm of mortals. But no agent ever operated on their own. Within that burning pyre, the azure eye of her commanding officer stared back at her.

"Report, Lieutenant." Replied General Vrilla.

"The operation is proceeding as scheduled." Efeu explained. "As you know, the prospect of reverse engineering any advanced technology has always enticed the surface world. For the past century, we have secretly been acting as a supplier to various companies and government agencies across the globe in exchange for food. Since the industrial revolution, the developed nations have grown dependent upon our inventions and innovations for their own day-to-day functionality. Their mythology tells of a creature called the 'cyborg'; a beast part flesh, part machine and neither half can survive without the other. If you will indulge me a slight sense of poetry, I feel that this makes a rather accurate metaphor for civilized society at this stage."

"I'm not interested in metaphors." Vrilla snapped. "Give me facts."

"Yes, General." The lieutenant answered, her tone more serious. "In this day and age, information, transportation, communication, production, education, entertainment, military operations and now even simple social interaction all involve the technology we provide in some form or another. Of course, the average folk all believe that such innovations were developed by their own kind and not by overmen, as if the average have ever innovated anything. Most interestingly, corporate profits and, as a direct result, national economies now require individual companies to supply consumers with superior technology than their rivals. Escalation being the first rule of conflict, we can expect offers for our services to increase in direct relation to the rising competition."

"Which means more food for our people." Vrilla concluded. "Well done, Lieutenant. You are very efficient."

"Thank you, General." Efeu said courteously. "I try."

"In your last report, you mentioned a problem with the increasing population. Update me on that situation."

"Of course." The lieutenant began. "The growth I have just described is, sadly, not indefinite. It is a bubble. It will become larger for a time, but it will inevitably pop. The reason is simple overcrowding. Due to the Untergeist's increased influence on the surface, governments are reluctant to enforce population control. Pity is regarded as a virtue rather than a weakness. The death of one for the benefit of many is seen as an atrocity. As a result, the number of hungry mouths is rapidly becoming greater than the number of edible rations needed to fill them, which naturally means..."

"I know what it means." The General barked. "It means that even if attempts are made to stretch the food supplies and distribute them fairly, it will still only be a quick fix. More people means that everyone has less."

"Precisely." Efeu explained. "A growing worldwide famine. Even in the richest countries, the increasing cost of basic necessities, from food to housing, is plunging more and more people into poverty. The dazzle of innovation may disguise it for now, but nobody can pull the wool over the public's eyes forever. It is only a matter of time before their people realize, just as ours did, that the most advanced of all computers is worthless to a starving man. When they reach that point, it is reasonable to assume that our days of plenty will be numbered."

"Yes." Vrilla added. "Two thousand years ago, we would have solved this problem by conquering new territory and claiming its resources as our own. But, ever since we let ourselves grow dependent on foreign markets, the high command is queasy about attacking a possible trading partner, even if it would never stand a chance against our military might."

"The Untergeist again." Efeu said. "The timid see conflict as something to end, the strong see it as something to win."

"That is so true." The General replied. "Even

our people are not free from the spirit of weakness. It is getting harder by the day to find anyone with true Atlantean fibre in their blood.”

Efeu sensed the frustration in her commanding officer's voice and suspected that she spied an opportunity. She would have to phrase her next statement carefully, since she was treading on very dangerous ground.

“What if I told you that a suitable amount of living space could be claimed as Atlantean territory on the surface world, complete with exploitable resources, and that it would actually improve trading operations for the high command?”

Vrilla was silent for a long time. With each second that passed, Efeu's pulse sped up. She clenched every muscle in her body in order to hide the fact that she was shaking.

“I'm listening.” The General said at last. Efeu breathed an undetectable sigh of relief.

“Well.” The lieutenant began. “As I've explained, the surface societies now require our technology in order to function. If this technology were to cease functioning simultaneously, all communication, trade, government and military operations would come to an immediate halt. As I'm sure you're aware, our engineers developed a kill switch as a precaution in case the surface world decided to wage war against us. With the push of one button, we could make the entire planet stop.”

“Have the surface worlders not realized this yet?” Vrilla asked.

“Heavens no!” Efeu laughed. “Only in this past century have they even wrapped their minds around nuclear fission. The terminology to describe how most of our science works doesn't even exist in any of their languages. Now, if such a global blackout *were* to occur and if it were to last for, say, about two hundred hours, a small faction of political activists, who are naturally sympathetic to our own cause, might stage a coup and seize control of one of the developed governments. From our current position, Germany could be taken easily. However, the land here produces a very low yield from an agricultural standpoint. But, if we were to expand and lay

claim to the likes of Austria, Hungary, Poland, Norway, Denmark and Iceland as well, then we would possess enough open farmland to feed our people independently of foreign markets for the next hundred years.”

“I think I see where this is going.” The General said. “The increased living space would allow the German population to continue expanding. Of course, the indigenous people of the surrounding countries would have to be either relocated or exterminated.”

“I'd let the high command decide which would be best.” Efeu said.

“Of course.” Vrilla replied. “And since this proposed state would be dependent on our military strength to sustain itself, it would effectively be an Atlantean territory, allowing us to seize the lion's share of its resources. We can then make it into the epicentre for technological progress on the surface and, with such a high demand, the world market will come begging for its scraps.”

“Precisely.”

Vrilla considered the proposal carefully.

“I can arrange the blackout. What supplies will be needed for this coup of yours?”

“Are the Mark-X Lances still being stored in that warehouse?” Efeu asked.

“Those old things?” Her commanding officer replied. “Of course. They haven't been used since the calls for disarmament began.”

“I shall need twelve of them, if the General would be so kind, of course.”

“I will make the requisition.” Vrilla said. “They should reach you in twenty minutes.”

The General's tone grew dark and her third eye filled with a rare seriousness.

“You realize that if this fails, we both stand to be cast into the Obsidian Realm.”

Efeu had considered this possibility. Every opportunity came with the chance of failure and, with it, disgrace. Disgrace for an overman was quite possibly the most fearsome fate of all, even more so than the death which they had conquered. Death would be a mercy compared to banishment to the Obsidian Realm. Yet, with every chance of disgrace, there was also the chance of greatness. Had her entire culture advanced to its supreme state by sailing only peaceful waters? No, not one civilization ever had. Thus, Efeu's course was clear to her.

"And if it succeeds, we shall be hailed as heroes." She answered. "After all, isn't victory the only difference between a hero and a villain? Remember, it is the victors who write the history books."

"Too true." Vrilla replied. "Alright, I want strategic updates as they happen and a progress report from you every hour. As of ten seconds ago, Operation Thule has begun."

"With all due respect, General." The lieutenant interrupted. "I have more experience with the surface worlders. I know their strategies. I know how they think. Isn't your commanding this operation a little unnecessary?"

Her words were greeted by a round of the General's bell-like laughter. The sound of her commanding officer's condescending mirth echoed throughout the vault, shaking the castle's ghosts from their darkened corners.

"Do you know what the problem is with intelligent people?" Vrilla asked. "You can never turn your back on them."

The General laughed again. The mockery in her voice was not lost on her subordinate.

"Over and out, Lieutenant. *Rahowa!*"

"Rahowa!" Efeu replied as the vision faded into non-existence. Efeu closed her third eye and returned to her surroundings. The pyre of hate was no longer visible to her, but she knew that it still burned as radiantly as ever. She called her commanding officer something vile as she rose from the marble floor and stretched. Her cigarette had nearly burnt out, so she tossed it aside and lit herself another. There was something else she craved to help wash down the taste of tobacco. She headed over to the spot where she had seen the inferno's glow a moment before and reached inside the unfinished pipe. Lucy had always kept a bottle of cognac hidden inside and, sure enough, it was still there.

Dear Lucy, she thought. *What would I do without her?*

Amongst her own people, Efeu was nothing special, just another number in an army of millions. But here on the surface, she was hailed as a superior race. In her own way, she did feel a certain affection for the two little apes that she had taken in. Not as friends or family, but in a style more akin to how a master feels about pets. They performed chores for her like loyal slaves. She would reward them when they were good and punished them whenever they misbehaved. Lucy was the more disciplined of the two, while Kikka often proved difficult to manage. Perhaps it was the mark of a stronger will to refuse submission. However, all living things submit in their own way, even Efeu herself. While she had been sure to provide for her charges, the Atlantean woman had not tasted food since the Iron Curtain fell. Like all of her people, her rigid coldness was developed to mask the constant pain in her belly. She held the bottle close to her face and studied her own reflection.

In Atlantis, only children grew their hair out. Being able to maintain a clean shaven scalp was regarded as a sign of self-discipline.

And no greater virtue existed in their culture.

As a little girl, Efeu had once been proud of her long, scarlet pigtails. Hair as red as the setting sun. Such a feature was rare, even in her homeland. However, the day eventually came when she'd had to part with it. It was when she was sixteen, the age when an Atlantean makes the step from mortal to overman. Efeu remembered the terror of it vividly. She and all who shared her birthday had been ordered to shave their heads, strip and submit themselves to a physical examination, which would determine their assigned duties within the Atlantean Reich. The vast majority of them were condemned to be used as test subjects in medical experiments. The secret to Atlantis' advanced technology was really no secret at all. Throughout history, scientific progress has always thrived in environments where experimentation was not limited by ethical codes or practices. Even on the surface, the current methods for treating exposure to extreme temperatures were developed by the Nazis and Japanese using decidedly unethical processes. They learned how much was enough by learning how much was too much. They discovered what worked by discovering what did not work. In this same manner, Atlantis annually sacrificed the weakest of her children to the betterment of science and, thus, the betterment of the Reich as a whole. In the process, the population growth was kept in check, natural selection remained in order and everybody was given an incentive to not be a branch of unproductive deadwood on the great tree of life. The overmen saw no atrocity in this blood offering to the gods of knowledge. With their land barren and food supplies dangerously low, it was seen as a charity. For in any scenario where human life is more abundant than the resources required to sustain it, the former will inevitably be regarded as having less value than the latter. Efeu had almost joined her comrades in the death camps. The examiner had hesitated briefly, his eyes focused on the red stubble that adorned her scalp, before sealing her fate with the stroke of a pen on a clipboard. Instead of dooming her to become a lab rat who would never taste the fruits of existence, he had assigned her to the military instead.

Condemning her to deprive others of those same fruits.

From there Efeu had joined The Wyrd Order and, under the command of General Vrilla, she was sent on black-ops missions in the surface world. But, in their endless quest to ward off their people's hunger pains, the Atlantean High Command would often send her to groom unknown dimensions for abuse.

Many thousands of years ago, the Reich had set about colonizing the infinite realms which lay beyond the veil. A great number of these brave new worlds now had their own civilizations living in secret beneath the roaring waves. All of them existed for the explicit purpose of acquiring food for the Fatherland. However, whenever she was sent to any of these colonies, there was something which disturbed her. Although some went by the name "Atlantis", others by the likes of "Thule", "Mu", "Lemuria" and "R'lyeh", the inhabitants of every single one of them believed that theirs was the true sunken kingdom and that all the others were the colonies. At first, she had merely laughed the idea away. But the seeds of doubt had been

planted in her mind. Many sleepless nights followed where she lay awake pondering if she too had been mislead as to the origin of her nation. Which of the many kingdoms was real? For that matter, had she ever even seen the true Atlantis?

Was there a true Atlantis?

There must be, she told herself. *Nature abhors a vacuum. Something had to have inspired the myth.*

She pictured a crowd gathered before a door which had never been opened, attempting to guess what lay on the other side. The imaginative souls within its ranks would envision all manner of impossible fantasies, whereas the unimaginative would visualize only the banal, if anything at all. While they might debate amongst themselves whose theory was the most probable, when the door was finally opened, the likeliest outcome would still be that all of them were dead wrong.

This was the mental predicament that Efeu now found herself in. Until the facts presented themselves, until the door opened, she would have to keep from projecting a palatable narrative onto the unknown. Belief and disbelief were both the traps of the lower tribesmen. A true Chieftain prescribed to neither, but dedicated their thoughts to contemplating possibilities. It was no easy task either. Remaining phlegmatic required self-discipline, a skill she had learned to value during her military career. To master the world, one must first master oneself. Efeu had a mental image of how she wished to be someday. Even though she knew that it was unrealistic, she strove towards it anyways, recognizing that to chase perfection was to never cease improving oneself. If she were to ever accept herself as she was, that would mean defeat. Thus, each morning, she put herself through a rigorous workout, the likes of which would terrify any surface world athlete. Within the borders of her homeland, meat, sweets, drugs and alcohol were all strictly forbidden. But whenever she left those borders behind, the decadence of foreign lands became constant temptations. Efeu had sworn off of candy and desserts quite successfully. However, she allowed herself to cheat on her people's vegetarian diet, reasoning that no species had ever risen to the top of the food chain by eating only roots and leaves. Indeed, from what she understood, the seafood she adored so much was actually necessary for a healthy brain. She never touched drugs, for the very idea of infecting her system with chemicals unnerved her. However, since her hyper-developed antibodies rendered her immune to the effects of tobacco, she saw no harm in cigarettes. She even felt that she did her best thinking while surrounded by cancerous fumes. Alcohol was proving to be a problem though. It affected clarity of thought and could become quite addictive. She had taken to leaning on the bottle during the Inquisition as a way of helping her cope with the unpleasantness of her duties. The barbarism which her superiors commanded her to oversee had left its mark. It was a stain upon her soul which could never be washed away.

For there was still a human in the superhuman.

Am I a barbarian? The lieutenant asked herself. She decided that she probably was. After all, civilized societies always hid behind jargon and double-talk for fear of offending their more delicate citizens. Frankness required a willingness to hurt the feelings of others. It took one who was comfortable with barbarism to do what they knew must be done.

It is not good. It is not evil either. It merely is.

Although some might have labelled Efeu a sadist, the truth was that she took no pleasure in watching others suffer. It was a duty and had to be carried out just like any other. Empathy was a privilege of those who had never been forced to fight for anything. Alcohol and its foul aftertaste had served to numb her to that particular emotion. It made her burdens no more pleasurable than before, but it did acclimate her to their repugnance. She could now order an execution as easily as she could order a drink. However, she was coming to realize just how dependant she had grown upon that same drink to keep her in this acclimated state.

Efeu gazed into the bottle of cognac. She could almost see the Untergeist waiting at the bottom, laughing at her weakness.

What would the dear General do if she were holding this bottle instead of I?

Efeu knew the answer. She could see it in Vrilla's platinum hair, which vanity had allowed her to grow out and comb to one side. How such an undisciplined individual could be a general astounded the lieutenant. Rumours circulated amongst the officers about how Vrilla had risen through the ranks not by virtue of merit, but as a result of an affair which she was having with someone in the higher echelons. Whether the rumours were true or not was irrelevant. So long as the possibility existed, Vrilla's performance would always be in question. In contrast, nobody doubted that Efeu had won her own position through hard work and perseverance. She recalled the night that she had received her promotion. Some of the other officers threw a party at her favourite pool, as it was no secret that swimming was her fondest off-duty activity. An admiral had even shown up to congratulate her. She never forgot how he had taken her aside and whispered an offer in her ear. An offer that sounded suspiciously like it might have been made to Vrilla once upon a time.

She never forgot her reply either.

"Many men work their entire lives to rise that high and never achieve it. Why should I be entitled to something that others must earn?"

At first, she was afraid that spurning an admiral's advances might have negative repercussions. But much later, she discovered that the same proposal was made to every new officer. It was, in actuality, one final test to make sure that they were truly deserving of their ranks and she had passed it with flying colours.

What would the dear General do if she were holding this bottle instead of I?

Efeu's crimson beads narrowed upon the drink in her hand. She raised it high and smashed the glass container against the floor. Its jagged shards stabbed up at her and dripped with now undrinkable flavours as she took a long drag from her cigarette. When the tip of her coffin nail glowed a bright orange, she flicked it into the sea of addiction. The ember lit the alcohol in a flash. Blue flame consumed the cognac, burning it away in a sapphire holocaust and lighting the eternal flame for all to see.

A Cheshire cat grin crossed Efeu's face while, somewhere in the cosmos, the Untergeist screamed in agony.

"You may outrank me, General. But you are still beneath me."

<u>Chapter 12</u>

"I am no monster. I am a miracle worker. I merely perform my miracles for my own people, rather than those who would harm them. Sadly, the surface worlders are too shallow to grasp what Dr Wolf and I created in the death camps. For we gave birth to a marvel and we did it using the most basic of all engineering tools, procreation.

You see, the human race lived a primitive lifestyle in a hostile environment for many, many centuries. Its survival was dependent on two factors; the availability of food, which had to be hunted in those days, and the presence of natural predators. In order to thrive in these conditions, humanity needed a stock that was strong enough to confront them. The fittest rose above the threats they faced, destroying whatever obstacles lay in their paths, while the weakest failed and died off. This culling of the herd ensured that only the most formidable genes would be passed on to future generations, increasing the race's overall value. This process has been dubbed 'natural selection'. However, as time passed, the environment changed. Humanity became so good at defending itself from its predators that it doomed most of them to extinction. Freed from the threats of a hostile environment, the human population expanded to ludicrous proportions. With no need to remain the fittest beast in the jungle, it saw no incentive to strengthen itself and became prey for the Untergeist. The now civilized race allowed itself to slip into lethargy. It pursued leisure instead of survival, pleasure instead of sustenance. Furthermore, weakness became regarded as something to pity rather than despise, prompting an abrupt halt to any culling of the herd. Disease, stupidity, obesity, deformity, laziness and genetic flaws became common, even

excused. With the law of natural selection violated, Mother Nature sought desperately for a way to restore her precious balance.

So, with our aid, she created a new animal.

Its camouflage is perfect. To all outward appearances, it is indistinguishable from the human race. Similarities in its DNA even allow it to mate with the surface worlders and spawn more its its own kind from their wombs. The only biological difference is a chemical reaction in its brain. Yet, that one difference is enough to change the course of history.

When this new overman was completed, Mother Nature took it aside and whispered in its ear.

'Go forth and hunt humanity!' She told it. 'Make the environment hostile once more! Thou art a cannibal tribesman. A headhunter. I have made thee bereft of empathy, bereft of morality's burden, so that thou may make the decisions that the human race cannot. The deaths of six million will mean nothing to thee. Thou shalt slaughter six million more if need be. The truly strong shall find a way to survive and procreate, the weak shall not, for survival is my sole measure of strength. They who cannot endure do not deserve to endure. I have also given thee a hunger for more than what is fair. Eat thy fill and let others scavenge. The human race has lived too well for too long and has grown soft from its decadence. Let them once again be forced to fight and strengthen themselves in the name of their continued existence. That is thy purpose in this world!'

And in that instant, Mother Nature gave this new being a very special name. She called it 'Psychopath'."

-Translated from Efeu's private journals

Casey felt nothing.

Vague shapes stalked around the perimeter of his barbed-wire fence. Although he recognized them as belonging to Kitty, Lucy and his mother, he no longer sensed their feelings radiating off of them. Their thoughts had ceased stabbing into his brain like leucotomes. The only thing filling his mind were the words of his Mephistopheles, which repeated themselves over and over...

Worshipped as a living god.

Those words lifted him and gave him purpose. He imagined himself as elevated above the average mortal, a life form superior to the sheep. Free from the machine.

A living god.

The ants came to him for pity, but he was now beyond their reach. They might as well have been dolls or mannequins.

Lifeless.

Unthinking.

Unfeeling.

"Casey." He heard one of the ants say. Its voice sounded like his mother's.

"Sweetie." She continued. "We have to go."

Casey said nothing. She had only ever called him "Sweetie" when she wanted him to do something for her. Her words fell on ears which heard only one phrase echoing again and again...

Worshipped as a living god.

"Casey please!" His mother called. "They're going to come back."

He did not reply.

Worshipped...

"I'm sorry I never told you about your father or your grandparents." She said. "I'm sorry I've lied. I know I... I've hurt you and I... I know that saying I'm sorry probably doesn't mean much. But I'm going to make things better. I really am sorry, Casey, and if you'll just come back to me, I'll make everything right. I was just so afraid that they'd take you away from me."

He heard her crying, but every tear she shed was a drop of cyanide.

"I just didn't want to be alone."

Worshipped...

"I love you."

...as a living god.

"You do not love." He replied. "You only possess. That is why my father returned to the sea. Thule was the only place where he could be free from you."

More tears followed. Casey felt nothing. He knew that his attitude was cold, but it was also necessary. Without it, she would have bled him dry.

Worshipped as a living god.

He'd had enough of her kind of "love". Once he had chased it, much like a believer chases Paradise. But he saw now that it was just another empty promise. Just another unattainable goal. He had no need of it. Without it lingering ahead, always slightly out of reach, he felt empty. What filled his heart in its place was hatred. It was the only thing he had left.

The only thing that she could not take away.

"I am Casey." He said.

I am KZ, he thought.

In his brain, he heard his grandmother's ghost whisper to him.

Join our tribe.

Fight our war.

Share our glory.

A *totenkopf* smile crossed Casey's face while the contents of his skull became a psychic storm.

Fight our war.

For too long, outside thoughts had immigrated into his mental territory. But now the borders were closed. It was the dawn of a new era, the first time in his life that he was not burdened by the thoughts of others.

And it was heavenly.

Chapter 13

"What is the mind? It is the so-called 'fifth dimension' described in popular culture (though not in mathematics), said to exist beyond the known spacial limits. First and foremost, every single one of us is a mind. For all effective purposes, the space inside our skulls may be referred to as five-dimensional space. Its understanding of the space outside is derived from information received through the sensory organs, which is then reconstructed within the brain as sounds, smells, flavours, sensations and images. Thus, what we see before us is not real space, but a representation of it in the virtual space of our imaginations.

A map in the war room of the soul.

The brain exists as an independent nation with the consciousness as its ruler. Through its allegiances, it helps to make up an empire larger

"We must leave this place." Kitty said in a faltering voice. She still felt dizzy, but the cloud of confusion was beginning to clear, if only a little. She hoped that meant that she was coming down from whatever poison they had pumped into her. Lucy kept giving her a smug stare. What could she be grinning about? Kitty noticed the death's head symbol on her ring and shivered.

I don't want to die here, she thought.

"I'm not leaving without my son!" Mrs Morgan snapped back. The raw anger in her voice made Kitty cringe. She found herself feeling strangely ashamed for upsetting the raven-haired architect. She thought that she understood how Casey must have always felt.

Afraid of shame.

Afraid of her.

Kitty tried to push her fear away, to rise above her shame and say what lay in her heart.

"He will not leave." She shouted back. "You heard him. We have to get out of here before that... that... *thing* returns."

"And let it have him?" Mrs Morgan yelled. Her dark eyes filled with venom. "Oh, I see. It's so easy to call yourself a friend when things are going well, isn't it? But now that things are going wrong, you just want to abandon him."

Kitty was stunned into silence. She cursed whatever drug was in her system for robbing her of her ability to think of any suitable replies. She had no snarky remarks, no witty comebacks. All she had was the feeling of something dirty in her blood, something that turned her brain into a fog. She didn't want the dirt to be inside her anymore. So, she projected it onto someone else.

"What about you?" She said. "I have seen the way you treat your son. And now you are surprised that he has turned against you?"

"I was only trying to protect him!"

"You were trying to protect yourself! Admit it, you hate him for being what he is. You are afraid of him and always have been. You think you can win him back by pretending to be nice? Well, it is too late now. If you need to find a reason for why he has turned away, look in a mirror."

Mrs Morgan simmered with suppressed rage. She attempted to contain herself, just as she always had in front of everyone except her private sacrificial lamb. Yet, the keg had been lit. A holocaust now exploded outwards, consuming everything in its path.

"How dare you?" She seethed. "You have no idea how hard it is to raise a child, watching him every minute to make sure that he doesn't grow into a monster. That takes dedication, something you obviously don't understand. But if you want to abandon him so badly, go right ahead. We don't need you. Go on! Get out!"

Efeu's hookah had lain undisturbed upon the marble floor all this time. Mrs Morgan snatched it and whipped the high-class pipe at Kitty's head. The girl's mop of pink hair ducked quickly as the Egyptian glass sailed over her and shattered against the wall.

"Get out!" Mrs Morgan screamed. Kitty felt swarmed by confusion in the face of so much rage. The sheer hate that radiated off of the old witch was like a dagger pointed at her heart. The haze was suffocating her. She had to get out. She had to break free. Kitty raced out of the *Obergruppenführersaal*, desperate to escape the madwoman's wrath. All manner of obscenities followed her down the marble hallways. She ran in search of an escape from the mental blur that gripped her.

But her search was in vain.

When she could no longer hear Mrs Morgan's shrieks, Kitty leaned against a window to rest for a moment. At least she could think better without all that noise ringing in her ears. She knew that she could use the secret passages to move about undetected, but questioned the wisdom of doing so knowing what was lurking inside them. If only she could concentrate, maybe she could think of a way out of here. But the castle cast long shadows, every one of which hid a potential threat. The entire place seemed like it had been built just to kill her.

She was caught inside of a giant deathtrap.

Chapter 14

"Every '-ism' is nothing more than the promotion of that concept to which '-ism' is affixed. Therefore 'racism' is the mere promotion of one's own race, 'Nationalism' is that of one's own national heritage and the four virtues that stem from it (see my thesis on race, creed class and kind in Chapter 5). National Socialism, or 'Nazism' as it is more commonly known today, should really be called 'National Corporatism'. State services are not 'socialized' (as the Left would have them). Nor are the privatized (as the Right would no doubt wish). Instead, they are turned into crown corporations. In place taxing the populace to fund handouts, the Nazi state offers its services at a price. The money from that pricetag then goes back into the public system and is used to improve the lives of all who live within the nation. The distinction must be drawn between NS (National Socialism) and MS (Marxist Socialism). While there are several overlapping themes between the two in regards to benefiting the poor and homeless, the central tenet of MS is the abolition of private ownership in favour of total state ownership. They preach this doctrine under the belief that it shall liberate the proletariat worker from effective slavery to their bourgeoisie employers. However, they fail to recognize that they are only shifting the underclass' servitude from the bourgeoisie to the state itself. NS rejects this fallacy outright. In my Fatherland, private ownership is supported, especially in regards to agricultural development. Free enterprise allows for competition. Competition fuels innovation, for one is constantly striving to outdo their rivals. Furthermore, it separates the strong from the weak, allowing the few truly exceptional individuals to rise to their rightful place at the top of the ladder. However, laws promoting productive business practices and condemning parasitical ones are given strict enforcement. For example, it is illegal to receive a form of income that is not the direct result of performing work. This effectively bans any unscrupulous banking and corporate activities. In this manner, business becomes the tool of the nation, rather than its master."

-Translated from Efeu's private journal

People were often surprised to learn that Otto Maurer was married. Most women found him so physically unappealing that such an idea sounded like a joke. However, Otto Maurer was married. It was a sleepless night for him and, as he lay wide awake, he appreciated his wife's presence next to him.

Let her rest, he thought. *Let her dream the blissful dreams of ignorance.*

Ignorance? Natassja was never ignorant. He had meant "innocence". Surely he must have. But what was innocence? Lack of knowledge or experience. Was that not the same thing as ignorance? Where was the line drawn between one and the other?

Was so-called "innocence" merely a glamorization of ignorance? A fresh coat of paint to make it appear more romantic?

Maurer rolled over in bed so that he could not see his wife's face. He did not wish to project such judgements onto the woman he loved. But the moment that he realized this, he wondered if he too was being ignorant. He shook the thought from his head, wishing that he could shake his thoughts of the castle just as easily.

"The only thing necessary for the triumph of evil is that good men do nothing."

Who had said that? He'd once been told that it was Burke, but had since learned that its source was unverified. It was just a saying without a speaker, floating through history and seducing the mind of the listener. But did that quote's elusive origins make its words any less true? Whatever was going on in the *Obergruppenführersaal*, Otto Maurer was letting it happen. Perhaps tomorrow he would wake up to find blood on his hands.

Perhaps. But tonight, he had the opportunity to stop that from happening. He could prevent the triumph of evil.

Carefully, so as not to wake his beloved, Maurer rose from the bed and dressed himself. He gave Natassja a goodnight kiss before leaving, possibly for the last time.

Nobody would ever accuse Otto Maurer of being strong-willed.

Let them begin to, he thought.

Chapter 15

*"**On the futility of 'freedom';** Who are we to liberate today? Is it the Romans who need rescuing from the Greeks? The Christians from the Romans? The Atheists from the Christians? The Chinese from the Atheists? The poor from the rich? The Left from the Right? The Right from the Left? Speak up, who is in need of deliverance? Say it quick, for I am growing awfully weary of hearing that same stale cry issued every generation or so as if it has never uttered at all. Every establishment began as a revolution. The rebels of yesterday always become tomorrow's tyrants.*

What is freedom? It is a myth which everyone is too frightened to debunk, for doing so would mean admitting to themselves that they can never be free. Tell me, what does the freedom fighter sacrifice in the name of his ideal? What does he compromise? Ha! Ironic, isn't it? If one makes no sacrifices, if one makes no compromises, then they are not truly fighting. Yet, the more they sacrifice, the more they compromise, the less free they become.

None of our misfortunes are new. Prejudice, war, superstition, fear, oppression and the like have dogged our steps since before the apes first gathered around the reassuring light of the bonfire in search of safety and community. Have you ever seen an ape? They are very childish animals. So, in the name of creating order amongst them, the ancient leaders invented ideals so that those over whom they ruled would work together willingly as a tribe. Concepts such as 'peace' and 'freedom' gave the apes something to live for. Over time, this tribe grew into a community, then a state, then an Atlantean Reich. Its existence was necessary for survival, for sustenance does not appear magically out of the ether. It exists in finite quantities. The struggle to produce and obtain sufficient amounts for oneself is perpetual. When an entire nation works to supply for its people, this chore becomes so much easier. However, for every mouth filled, another must still go hungry. So long as humanity needs to eat, it shall be a slave to the environmental, social and innovative factors which act as suppliers for its daily bread. So you see, submission has always existed. Freedom never has. What is it that the quantum theorists like to say? 'If something can happen it inevitably does'. Tell me then, why has true freedom never come to be? Or true equality? Or true peace? The answer is obvious, is it not? These ideas may warm hearts, but they cannot fill empty bellies.

Chase freedom and you might as well chase the end of a rainbow."
-Translated from Efeu's private journals

No matter how hard she tried to tiptoe through the secret passageway, Kitty's footsteps still seemed to echo. She swore silently, cursing her feet for being so loud. She thought that maybe if she had succeeded in sticking to that diet which Sarah Lin had convinced her to try, her feet probably wouldn't be so heavy now. Then at least they would be making less noise.

Sarah's face appeared to her through the haze. The fever dream came like a bolt of lightning. Why didn't she call her best friend? Sarah could do something. Sarah could get help!

Kitty felt around in her pocket for her cellphone. Her cognitive functions began to cloud again, but she just kept digging. She explored the darkness of her pocket just as she explored the darkness of the hallway. She could see nothing in either case, but guided herself by touch. She had memorized the layout of these passageways, having used them to disappear from the outside world for hours at a time. But now she felt her memory failing her. The path to freedom was not so certain anymore. Should she turn right, left, or just keep going straight? Kitty was not sure. She wasn't sure about her cellphone either. Her pocket felt like a doorway to another dimension. Every inch of space that both her toes and fingers wandered through was just an unknown abyss. It didn't help that she could never be certain where the next attack would come from. Every inch of wall space was a potential doorway to death. Even the ceiling had to be watched. It would be far too easy for a claw to reach down and hook her throat.

Using her fingers as eyes, she probed the darkened passageway. She moved just a little bit at a time, fearful that haste might lead her astray. However, the haze prevented her from having any clear idea of her bearings. Thankfully, her small hands found the contours of something in her pocket. Her cell! She had found the freedom which she so desperately craved. But the moment that she pulled it out, the first thing that she saw was a blue eye staring at her from the screen.

"Computers have brains too." It said, as if whispering in her subconscious. *"They're even easier to influence than human brains. Did you really think that you could escape from us?"*

Kitty threw the device away and ran. She didn't know where she ran to and she didn't care either. She just wanted to get away from that eye. But the more she ran, the more she saw it everywhere. It was in the walls. In the ceiling. In the floor.

In her heart.

There is no way out of here, she thought. Kitty took deep, long breaths to try and calm herself.

There has to be a way out. There has to be.

She tried to think. One of these passages would have to lead to the eastern wing. It would be a long, perilous walk to the castle's main entrance, but she was running out of alternatives very quickly.

You're doing okay, she told herself. *Just a little further...*

Kitty's fingers led the way through the blackness once again. The roughly hewn edges of brick stabbed at her skin, as if the castle itself were out to murder her. However, she persevered, knowing that escape lay at the end of the tunnel.

It had to.

At last, her hands found what they sought. This door would take her to liberty. She would just have to get downstairs and then she'd be home free. She felt around for the switch that would open the secret hatchway, anxious for the nightmare to end.

Kitty brushed against something wet.

Something soft.

Flesh.

Oh God.

She recoiled in horror from the touch of a human corpse. One that wore rimless glasses.

"Papa." She whispered. Her father's body was crucified before her, draped like a curtain across her exit to freedom. Kitty gagged in disgust at what had been done to him. He was a scarecrow, meant to frighten her from passing this way. Her revulsion gave way to sadness that a person could be treated so wastefully. That a life could be seen as undesirable.

"Papa." She said. "I'm sorry."

Her father said nothing. His hanging body offered no forgiveness. Nothing to ease her weighing conscience. If there was a Heaven, perhaps his spirit really had gone there. But this shape before her was just a shell now. No apologies to him would grant her salvation from her own guilty heart.

It was just one more unattainable goal.

With a heavy burden on her soul, she pushed herself past the grisly effigy and felt around for that blasted switch. At last, she found something small and round, which she turned anxiously. She watched the door ease open, worried that there might be someone on the other side. Moonlight poured into the passageway, illuminating her father's lifeless eyes. Their empty stare would haunt her for the rest of her days. She forced the bile in her throat downwards and peered out of her hiding place. The adjoining room was a large dining area that was apparently under Mrs Morgan's renovations. The long tables were draped with transparent sheets in order to protect them from the fresh paint. The fumes from it assaulted her nostrils, but at least they were all that she smelled.

Kitty slid into the unfinished room and closed the door behind her with what registered in her brain as a loud boom. The haze returned as it thundered through her skull, followed by the sound of jackbooted footsteps. Their marching was like an approaching storm. The noise came from everywhere at once. The armies of death were coming for her. They shined a spotlight in her face, blinding her. All that Kitty could see was a uniformed silhouette standing sentry with a lamp in his hand.

"What do you think you're doing here." The shadow said in German. Kitty's vision cleared slightly and the figure came into focus.

"A security guard." She said. Her voice was weak from staying quiet for so long. "You're really a security guard?"

He had light brown hair and he needed a shave, but he was a welcome sight. One unclouded look at him told Kitty that she had reached safety at long last.

"Please help me." She pleaded. "They killed my father. They're after me."

As she spoke, a chill draft blew in from the hallway. She would not have given it a second thought except that it carried a scent which made her blood run cold.

Almonds.

Genocide was coming and its cruel finger pointed at her.

"Oh God!" She cried. "Please get me out of here. They're going to kill me!"

The guard studied her face, as if attempting to discern her sincerity. The Zyklon-B scented wind blew stronger and a purple glow emanated from Kitty's pocket. She reached inside and retrieved the amethyst crystals. They shone with a supernatural, violet light, reacting to the presence of evil.

"They're coming." She said. The guard's eyes widened at the sight. He lifted his hand-held radio to his lips.

"Ingrid, Hans." He barked. "We have a situation in the northeast corridor. Second floor. I think this has to do with what Mr Maurer told us about."

A warm, reassuring smile appeared on his face. That smile parted the clouds and let the sun shine through.

"Don't worry, *fraulein*." He told Kitty. "We're going to get you to safety."

Relief and happiness filled Kitty's soul.

"Thank you." She answered him with utter elation. She felt safer already.

Together, they stepped into the hallway. The guard remained alert as he made sure that their path was secure. However, the smell of bitter almonds kept growing more potent. Kitty knew that there could be no security from the walking concentration camp who was its source. The dogs of war were on her trail and nothing would stop them from tasting her flesh. She could practically feel them snapping at her heels as her rescuer led her down the corridor. An elevator waited for them at the far end. They would have to take it in order to get downstairs to the reception room.

If only they could make it in time.

Kitty pushed the button the moment that it came within reach, but could still sense the Atlantean war machine following her. The smell was practically choking her now and the lift was moving ever so slow.

Kitty jumped as the guard's radio came alive suddenly. She scolded herself for acting so silly, but decided that her behaviour was perfectly reasonable under the current conditions. A woman's voice came through the cloud of static on the other end.

"I'm almost there." A female guard said. A few more seconds of silence followed, ending with an exasperated sigh.

"I see the intruder." She said. "It's another one of those skinheads."

Kitty tensed up.

"Tell her to get out of there." She said. "That thing isn't just a thug. It isn't human."

The sound of gunfire ripped through the night. Each shot felt like a nail being hammered into a coffin. After three or four of them, they stopped as abruptly as they had begun.

"Ingrid?" Kitty's protector said into his radio.

Ingrid did not reply.

The fox had overcome the rabbit.

Kitty saw beads of sweat drip down her

rescuer's brow. His hard eyes melted into worry and fear.

"Hans." He said. "Are you there?"

"Almost." A man's voice replied. "I'm running as fast as I... Oh God!"

"What is it?"

"It's Ingrid. She's... Oh my God... Her guts are... Someone ripped her guts out."

Silence claimed the radio once more.

"Hans, come in." The guard commanded. His comrade did not answer. Instead, a voice that Kitty dreaded came over the receiver. One that spoke very poor German and made the crystals glow brightly.

"Here, Kitty, Kitty." It taunted. "Are you there, Kitty?"

"Who is this?" The guard said.

"Let me talk to girl, caveman!" The voice hissed.

"And if I don't?"

A weak voice came over the radio. It said nothing, but whimpered in pain.

"Hans." The guard said. "What did she do to you? Are you alright?"

Before Hans could answer, the *fraulein* returned to the airwaves. She spoke with a confidence that chilled Kitty through and through, as if she knew that she had already won.

"In your language, word is 'inquisitor'." She said. "My people have vehicles codenamed 'Inquisitors'. They are portable torture chamber. Can appear anywhere on command. Our biologists make bacteria for interrogation. Inject it into stomach. It then eat intestines from inside. Eat whole person sometimes. I see it once. Subject last for nine days, hurt whole time. Hurt bad. Subject beg to die."

The cruel voice giggled, like a schoolgirl sharing a rumour in the locker room.

"Imagine it! Iron chair, Judas cradle, wire jacket, waterboard, even electroshock equipment. I send for Inquisitor. It come. Then this man beg to die too."

"You're bluffing." The guard said. "Nobody has those kinds of resources."

"And if I tell truth, do you want this man's hurt on your conscience?"

Kitty's protector stood in silent indecision. She watched him weigh his chances before concluding that he was simply not meant for gambling. With a submissive hand, the guard passed the radio to his young charge.

"What do you want?" Kitty asked.

"I want you, Kitty." The demonic voice said. "I have job for you. Meet me in vault in ten minute. Understand?"

"Yes." Kitty answered.

"Good." The *fraulein* continued. "Now put caveman back on."

The guard took his radio back.

"Yes?" He asked.

"Now, listen carefully." The voice said in a condescending tone. "Do not contact either police or your employer. Instead, escort girl to vault, at gunpoint if you must. Then, keep snout out of my feeding trough. Understood?"

"Perfectly." He muttered.

"You had better." The voice snapped. *"Rahowa!"*

The radio burst into a storm of static, then went dead. But the crystals did not stop glowing.

<u>Chapter 16</u>

"Are we truly such devils? The surface world Shamans preach of our wickedness, like nervous hausfrauen warning their children to beware of the goblins.

'Yes, Hansi, remember to eat your vegetables, brush your teeth, say your prayers and vote for the people mother tells you to. If you're not a good little boy, the Nazis who live in your closet will take all your rights away.'

Speaking as a Fascist (and I would rather be a Fascist than a mule with carrots called 'peace', 'freedom' and 'equality' perpetually dangled just out of my reach), the term is used awfully loosely on the surface. I keep hearing that one movement or another is following in Hitler's footsteps, yet I see no concentration camps. No mass graves. No crematoriums with fires running twenty-four hours a day.

We have become akin to witches, though not in the way that our enemies would paint us.

The road to Wewelsburg Castle was steeped in darkness. The headlights on Maurer's car did not dispel the ever encroaching shadows, but merely pushed them back to a safe distance. As the director drove, he could still feel them reaching out at him, attempting to snatch his soul. They could not get him. Not this time. But his convictions would not stop them from trying. He could see the castle in the distance, silhouetted against the starlit sky. That same silhouette seemed to grow before his eyes. The north tower rose out of the earth. He watched as it became tall and pointed, like a giant hooded man. It was an evil king with no tolerance for any act of defiance. Especially his.

Maurer pressed his foot on the accelerator. He would not be intimidated by this shadow again. However, the living darkness was in no mood for insolence. It reached down from its castle and cast its hand over the car. The director felt its icy fingers clenching his throat. They squeezed his windpipe, blocking off the airflow. His face turned purple from lack of oxygen. Maurer could feel his consciousness slipping. He had to stay awake. He had to stop...

The car swerved to the side of the road and smashed into a waiting oak tree. The director of Wewelsburg Castle sat slumped behind the wheel. His eyes were wide open, but his heart would never beat again.

With its mission accomplished, the living darkness returned to the castle to serve its mistress.

<u>Chapter 17</u>

*"**The Six Gates Of Fear;** Before humanity knew how to love, it knew how to fear. It grew so deathly afraid of its fears that it taught itself to love so that it would not have to bear the constant burden of this oldest and most primal of all emotions. But when the species found that love only spurned it, it then learned to bury its fear through other emotions. First, its terror was channelled into anger. Then, that anger was projected onto others, transforming it into hate. The specific targets of hate have been different for every tribe, but the pattern has always been the same. All ways of thinking have an ideal to rally for and an anti-ideal to rally against, thus no philosophy is without a scapegoat. How do we begin to scapegoat? We begin by searching for 'the one problem', the single cause of every relevant issue. Then, we must construct a model of how it operates, so that we may demonstrate to others the extent to which it affects their lives. The details of this model are unimportant so long as it portrays 'the one problem' as widespread and frightening. In order to accomplish this, it must tap into the public's own fears. Your propaganda may then exploit these fears in the styles listed below.*

*(**Note:** The following list is by no means complete or comprehensive. It is merely a starting point for future innovators in the fine art of*

horror.)

Shock: *If we wish to define this first and weakest type of fear, we may describe it as 'an unpleasant surprise'. The most typical example of this is to show your subject the damage caused by the scapegoat's 'crimes'. While effective as a gateway to the other, stronger types, it has little value beyond that. As a result, it should be employed as sparingly as possible. Understand that every time you shock your subject, they develop a tolerance to being shocked. Thus, overuse of this tactic will desensitized your target audience to your cause. Keeping the attention of a desensitized subject will require bigger and bigger shocks, until they have become thoroughly numbed to everything you are trying to say. 'Shocktivism' is a form of political activism that attempts to draw attention to an issue through the use of shocking messages. However, this will inevitably prove counterproductive to any tribe's long-term goals. The scenario that I've already illustrated is not the only reason either. Such base tactics tend to appeal primarily to the bad seeds of the movement, for no tribe is without its black sheep. Shocktivism attracts these social miscreants like flies to a cadaver, enabling them to the very forefront of the cause. The eggs they lay within it will only hatch into flesh-eating maggots.*

Creepiness: *The 'fear of that which is different'. Perhaps a more accurate definition would be the 'fear of unexplained abstraction'. This is the building block of prejudice. It begins with an aesthetic which the subject finds pleasing. When 'X' does not conform to this aesthetic, as something inevitably must, the shock (see above) triggers a response akin to the classic 'fight or flight'. One scenario is that the subject will choose to 'fight' their own lack of knowledge by attempting to understand 'X', gaining a better grasp of the world in the process. The other scenario is that they will choose to 'flee' by dismissing 'X' as frightening or repulsive. An aesthetic can be contradicted by any number of things; the unusual, the 'out of place', the taboo, the unappealing (example; 'he looks creepy') or even the alien (examples; unfamiliar cultures,*

foreign races, unconventional sexual preferences, etc). When one fears 'X', it become the enemy. Fear gives way to hostility. Hostility to aggression. Thus, that which is creepy makes the perfect scapegoat.

Eeriness: *Not so much a fear in itself, but rather a method for reinforcing the subject's fears. Eeriness is an atmosphere created by employing iconography, archetypes and concepts with which your target audience already possesses strong negative associations (examples; murder, rape, prison, war, chains, mind control, any imagery associated with death or the graveyard, etc). Your propaganda should never cease to juxtapose these hated concepts with your chosen scapegoat, as it will prompt your subject to associate them with each other unconsciously.*

Suspense: *The 'fear of the future', spawned by uncertainty as to whether or not it will be favourable. Consider what Alfred Hitchcock called the 'time bomb'; a threat that will have disastrous consequences (not right now, but very soon) which the drama's principle players are unaware of, but the audience knows is ever present. The subject is then forced to sit and sweat with the knowledge that this 'time bomb' might 'go off' if the heroes do not do something about it quickly. Storytellers apply this scenario to both fiction and real life. The threat posed by the scapegoat is the 'bomb' and the public are the 'heroes' who must prevent the metaphorical 'explosion', if the tribe can only warn them in time. Ironically, the longer that the imaginary bomb goes without detonating, the greater the level of anticipation surrounding it. It is necessary for the tribe to generate a feeling of suspense. For when the enemy threat hangs constantly over the subject's head, any course of action used to counter it seems justified.*

Paranoia: *The 'fear of trust'. Unless one is truly psychic, they can never know what thoughts lie in the heads of others. This lack of knowledge can be exploited by stating the previous sentence simply and plainly. Then, once the seeds of doubt have been sown, they can be allowed to grow and bear fruit by the mere power of suggestion. The key here is to cultivate suspicion by conveying the* *theory that the problem posed by the scapegoat is larger than the subject realizes. Perhaps it is a literal criminal conspiracy. Maybe it is simply a fundamental flaw in how the establishment works, triggering a toxic way of thinking in those who put their faith in it. Or maybe it is just 'their' nature to think and act violently (but not 'ours', never 'ours'). Every slight suffered shall then be interpreted as evidence of a systemic problem, rather than the natural trials of day-to-day survival. Anyone with a different opinion will be seen as an enemy agent. When your subject believes that the problem is outside and utterly rampant, they will project mistrust upon anything with a passing resemblance to the scapegoat.*

Disturbance: *By far the most powerful of all fears. It is the 'fear of being contradicted' or perhaps, more bluntly, the 'fear of being wrong'. From the moment of birth, the sentient mind begins forming an understanding of the world around it. Eventually, this understanding is taken for granted and becomes a belief. However, when that belief is challenged, uncertainty superimposes knowledge. Self-worth is questioned as the known becomes unknown once more. The subject's mind then scrambles to maintain its beliefs so that it will not be faced with the realization that it was wrong about everything. It will rationalize and justify its own behaviour, no matter how foolish, then channel its fear into unequalled rage at the offending party. Disturbance is the ultimate terror for it perpetuates all other forms of fear and is, in turn, perpetuated by them.*

-Translated from Efeu's private journals

Entrance to the vault was barred by a large, metal gate. Kitty found it reminiscent of the portal to a cemetery. Perhaps the similarity was intentional. She could practically feel the ghosts of the Third Reich's fallen heroes reaching out to exterminate her.

The door was usually kept locked. However, as the girl put her hand on it, the iron bars creaked open with a dreadful sound. Both she and the guard scrunched their noses in disgust as a cool draft blew into their faces, poisoning their nostrils with bitter almonds.

Kitty struggled to peer through her mental fog. It was no easy task. The haze was spread about the tomb like mist, blanketing it in confusion. She spied Efeu sitting on the edge of the eternal flame, humming blithely to nobody in particular. The Atlantean had changed out of her evening wear and into her work clothes. A tight red wetsuit with purple leggings hugged her athletic body, its high collar decorated with her country's insignia. There were even a pair of silver medals on her bosom.

She did not even look at either Kitty or her protector as they stepped into the mausoleum. She just stared off into space, lost in introspection. For the first time, the girl could see her enemy's face, but wondered if she wasn't hallucinating. Dagger-sharp cheekbones, a proud chin, nightmare eyes and a highly philosophical brow were all set like diadems in a short-haired *totenkopf*. Everything about the Thule Society's *kommandant* seemed to radiate power. If she gave a command, Kitty would have to struggle not to obey it.

"Where is Hans?" The guard demanded. His gun was trained over Efeu's skull and Kitty sensed an itchy trigger finger.

"Nice man." Efeu replied. "He hurt. I could not watch. He not hurt anymore."

Anger flared in the guard's face. The spirits of dead comrades urged his hands to fire a lethal shot. One bullet in that red-headed scalp and they would be avenged.

Kitty did not see Efeu move. When the gunfire flashed, the *fraulein* was simply not sitting where she had been. As the bullet hit only empty air, the living blitzkrieg sprang at them with superhuman speed. The girl's protector tried to get another shot in, but it was already too late. There was a quick blur of motion, a flicker of Atlantean claws and the guard's head was torn from his body.

Kitty gagged at the sight. However, she knew that she could not let the crimson spray distract her. Her thoughts still weren't clear, but they were coherent enough to recognize that mortal weapons could not hurt this elegant yet terrible creature. She fished into her pocket and withdrew a handful of amethyst. The crystals glowed with a supernatural, purple light. They cast the shadows away and created room for hope again.

Efeu remained a mountain. Her ivory face betrayed neither fear nor surprise. Not even the sensation of being impressed. Just a cool impassiveness.

She did not swipe the crystals from Kitty's hand. She swiped the hand from her wrist.

Numbed by whatever venom had polluted her system, the girl felt no pain. She felt no shock either, just disbelief. She stared at the red stump that now decorated the end of her arm. Her brown eyes then fell to the severed fist on the floor. Her life's fluid joined that of her protector in a crimson pool. If she did not act quickly, Kitty knew that she would bleed to death.

The *fraulein* closed her matching rubies and a third eye opened on her forehead. It was the same eye that had been haunting Kitty through the haze. So blue. So deep. The girl gazed into that sapphire and a will more powerful than anything she had ever felt before seized her consciousness. Reality seemed to dance and blur as the red water poured from her body. Time became fragmented. Life was but a dream.

The castle's occult technology came to life with a low hum. It cleared the fog from Kitty's mind, the toxin from her body. When every last bit of the haze had disappeared, she saw that her hand had been regrown. However, a symbol was now tattooed on the palm.

The *totenkopf.*

A gentle voice spoke in her mind.

You now owe your life to me. That kind of debt can only be payed with servitude.

Kitty fell to her knees as the realization sank in.

Join our tribe.
Fight our war.
Share our glory.

The girl curled up in a foetal position, wishing that everything would just go away. Like the other members of the Thule Society, she too now bore a sign of ownership. The death's head had been branded on her right hand.

And the mark of the Black Sun was branded on her soul.

I don't belong to anybody, she told herself. *I have my own dreams. I'm going to move to LA and become a rockstar someday. I am my own person.*

The uniformed figure knelt next to her. Like God speaking to Moses on the mount, she leaned in and whispered into the girl's ear. Although she spoke in Runespeak, Kitty now found herself able to understand the foreign language.

"You're nobody." Efeu said. "You're something for us to experiment on. We'll infect you with a lethal bacteria just to see if we can cure it. We'll mutilate a part of you just to see if we can heal it. We'll cut off pieces of you just to see if we can reattach them. Then, we'll dissect you so that we can better understand how the process affected your body. But we won't stop there. Oh, heavens no! We'll make soap from your fat, leather from your skin and formaldehyde from your spinal fluid. Then, after we've stripped your corpse of everything valuable, we'll stuff you in an oven and use your ashes as fertilizer. Because that is all any of you truly are. You are nothing but cattle to be herded and exploited at best, exterminated completely at worst. You may see yourself as something revolutionary, but in my eyes you're still just a primitive savage."

"I wouldn't be so sure of that." Kitty argued. "We've come a long way."

"No you haven't." The *fraulein* giggled. "It is the curse of those who live upon the surface that they can never see beyond it. You aren't as low tech as you were three thousand years ago, but is a primate more advanced just because it owns a shinier toy? Would giving cellphones to the Romans have made them any less barbaric? No, child, technology is not a sign of higher development. In fact, you should take me as living proof that it only makes the subversive elements more efficient. You see, the problem is not science. It doesn't lie in any beliefs, values, systems, 'wings' or the multitude of other external factors that your people wish to project blame upon. Wake up and smell the Zyklon-B. The problem is you! You, the human animal. Do you realize that your bodies have remained unchanged since prehistoric times? Prehistoric times! Tell me, how can any race lay claim to progress when, biologically, it is still thinking with caveman brains? That is why we have brought you here. You are going to bear witness to something which I have been working on since the days of Hitler. The birth of the New Man."

"The New Man?" Kitty replied. "You mean... Casey?"

Efeu spent a moment in solemn silence.

"I believe that, in your culture, it is customary for grandparents to spoil their grandchildren." She said. "Do you know what I wish? I wish I could have spoiled the boy. His sister has been a little darling, but his own life was always out of my hands. However, he is now sixteen, a legal adult in my Fatherland, and has every right to walk away from his mother's custody. So, I shall make up for lost time by giving him a gift that none of your ideals can ever dream to."

She gave a wicked giggle.

"And you realize that this why you've lost the war for his heart, don't you? Rest assured, he will turn his back on you and not because of any spells or brainwashing either. He will do it simply because we offer him a satisfaction that you never could."

The sound of marching feet became audible. It began as a distant tremor, then escalated into thunderclaps that echoed through the crypt. Kitty watched as the punk woman raced into the chamber. Once, she had thought that this dirty creature was the more fun-looking of the twins. But now, the sight of that unwashed hair and those faded clothes filled her with disgust. Even her actions now seemed pathetic. The tramp grovelled before her mistress like a frightened child, as if she was even more terrified of the Atlantean than Kitty was.

"F-fraulein." She stammered. "M-mein kommandant. We have found something strange outside. Canisters of some sort."

"Are there twelve of them?" Efeu asked. Her subordinate nodded and the *fraulein* gave her a smile like an owner gives to their dog.

"Good." The lady in scarlet said. "Be a dear,

Kikka, and have them brought in."

Kikka nodded a second time and scrambled out through the gate. When she returned, the shadows followed her. The living darkness descended upon the vault and the ghosts of the Thule Society came bearing gifts for their mistress; a set of large containers made from a strange, bronze alloy.

"I've never seen anything like these before." The punk said. "We've tried opening them, but nothing works. And those markings,... that metal,..."

"The markings are the insignia of the Atlantean applied science division." Efeu explained. "The metal is orihalcon. It is rare on the surface, but quite common in my Fatherland. As for the locks, they are fine-tuned to my people's DNA and I'm afraid they won't respond to yours."

With the air of a professional, she placed a hand on either side of one of the containers and spread her taloned fingers wide. The lid began glowing red and a low hum filled the air.

"Upina." Efeu commanded in Runespeak. Kitty watched in awe as the collection of otherwordly vessels opened. From out of them rose twelve large blades that stabbed upwards at the stars, as if they were Atlantis' war spears rising out of the sea. The *fraulein* lifted one effortlessly. With a single hand, she gave her new toy a couple of trial swings and smiled in satisfaction.

"Do you recognize this, Kikka?" She asked.

"It's the lance of Longinus." The punk replied. "The Spear of Destiny. But how did you..?"

Efeu giggled at her knight's naivete.

"This is not the artifact that Hitler seized from Austria." She explained. "His was a Mark-VII battle lance, an Atlantean invention, given to the Norse kings as a goodwill gift by my predecessor. The vikings spread the legends of how it was Odin's own spear, Gungnir. But then, Christian missionaries reinterpreted it as the weapon which impaled Jesus in an effort to convert the Norse to their own Pseudo-Hebrew faith."

She finished that last sentence with a bitter

sneer.

"For a mortal like Hitler, it could only unlock a small fraction of his potential." She continued. "He had enough latent psychic ability that gave him limited 'powers'. But this lance,... this is a Mark-X! Far more advanced than the one he possessed and capable of unleashing a much greater force from its bearer."

Kikka held out expectant hands, hopeful that such a divine gift might be granted to her. However, her mistress was not in the habit of giving to beggars. Efeu turned up her nose at the dirt-ridden vagabond and recoiled from her pitiful gesture.

"You wouldn't even be able to lift one of these off the ground." The *fraulein* spat. "No, these shall be wielded by stronger hands than yours."

A stillness blanketed the tomb as Kitty watched the twelve shadows gather in a ritualistic circle around their mistress. They saluted the Atlantean, a representative of their superior dream race, raising their hands high into the heavens.

"*Rahowa!*" The hooded ghosts cried.

"*Rahowa!*" Efeu replied, accepting their praises. She gestured to the spears with a clawed finger and bestowed her blessings upon her worshippers. Eleven of the *Einherjar* accepted their gifts with humility and grace. The twelfth stood before his ivory-carved idol and received his boon directly from her hand. In Kitty's eyes, he was like Arthur accepting Excalibur.

"*Fraulein.*" She heard him say. "The police have dispatched two units to the castle."

Efeu seemed troubled by this news for a second, but only for a second. A cruel smile formed on her lips as her highly evolved brain formulated a plan.

"Alright." She said. "If the dogs of war come howling at our gates, let us show them how the Thule Society welcomes visitors."

She crossed her talons in salutation.

"*Rahowa!*" She shouted.

"*Rahowa!*" The ghosts replied. They raised their spears high like cavemen and chanted that Atlantean word over and over again, imagining that it gave them strength.

"*Rahowa!*"

"*Rahowa!*"

"*Rahowa!*"

Kitty watched the ritual in terror. A part of her brain still felt that she had to do something, that this hellishness needed to stop.

But what could she hope to do?

She was just a cog in a machine now.

And she would live and die at her mistress's behest...

Chapter 18

"***The Othil Rune;*** *Natural selection is the means by which evolution strengthens us. A race that cannot survive the threats in its environment dies out while another, which fortifies and adapts itself to these threats, lives on. This ensures that only the strongest genes are passed on to future generations. Othil denotes nobility within the persevering races. It is two life runes combined, revealing to us that, in order to rise to an 'Alpha' position, one must strive to live with the strength and cunning of two. Wear Othil in order to elevate yourself through the hierarchy of fitness. By taking what it represents to heart, nature will then select you for survival and lift you above the meek, who lack true strength and require others to fight for their survival. Thus, it is nature's will that the tender should be dominated by the forceful. Indeed, how is it even possible that one particular group can be chained to a servant class for centuries if they are not innately frailer than their masters?"*

*-**Translated from Efeu's private journals***

Ivy is an exotic yet highly invasive species of plant. Its long, creeping vines snake their way through forests, spreading seeds wherever they go. While not actually parasitic, its aggressive nature has been known to kill trees by either shielding them from the life-giving sunlight or crushing them beneath the force of its own weight. Some people also believe that dreaming of ivy is an omen of division and strife.

Such were the vines that crept over Wewelsburg Castle. They had grown rampantly over the ancient fortress, clutching it like a raised fist. During the daylight hours, they blocked the sun from shining upon it.

And we all know what lurks in the places where no ray can penetrate.

It was from these places that the vines spread. First came the blackout. In only an instant, everything made by human hands ceased to function and the entire planet was brought to its knees.

With the way for their coming cleared, the twelve shadows stretched out from Wewelsburg's most hidden crevices. They grew uncannily long, casting themselves over the country and blanketing every inch of fertile soil. Each of them lay claim to one of the surrounding nations and possessed the minds of their respective leaders. The spears of destiny struck the politician's hearts, splitting them in twain and creating an irreparable divide. From those wounds leaked an almond-scented breeze, which carried its poison across the land. The people breathed deeply of this air and its venom reached their brains, splitting them in half as well. It began with simple resentment. But, with each breath, it escalated. It spawned anger, then vengeance and, ultimately, hate. Each side condemned the violent actions of the other while celebrating its own. Although a few preached for reconciliation, the conflict was inevitable resolved in the same manner that every other has ever been; with sheer force and the willingness to use it. When the possessed succeeded in quelling their enemies, they joined their powers together to form a Reich of Darkness. Membership to this unholy kingdom was open to anyone who supported its ideals. All who opposed these ideals were branded as enemies of the state. Thus, the new way was established. The twelve phantom kings built their thrones from the bones of their most hated foes. Remnants of the old civilization were set ablaze to make room for the cities of the future. Many objected, but met their ends impaled on Atlantean blades.

For the world had grown soft.

As the mark of the Black Sun was elevated above the planet, all the creatures of fantasy, from the elves and faerie folk to the werewolves and vampire broods, fled to their sanctuaries. The dawning holocaust dogged their steps as they flew from the world of mortals, never to return. For there was to be no room for them in the Age of Overmen.

It was a night that all the realms would remember forever.

The night that love finally failed.

Chapter 19

"Only the weak live in fear of dystopia. Indeed, only the weak would need to fear it for they alone die out in hostile environments, whereas the fittest adapt to their surroundings and survive."
-Translated from Efeu's private journals

An orange glow seeped through the windows of the *Obergruppenführersaal*, illuminating the chamber with the radiance of a planet on fire. Casey could sense his mother's terror as she looked out into the world she once knew. All the lights of the town had blinked out completely and huge, billowing clouds of smoke rose into the starless sky. Although she guarded what lay in her heart, her son's gift saw right through her disguise.

There was no help coming.

There was no help left to come.

Mrs Morgan sat on the cold floor and tried playing with the buttons on her cellphone. However, just like the land outside, the machine was dead. She tossed the now useless gadget aside and buried her head between her legs. All communication was severed. There was nothing left that she could do except mourn.

"The police will come soon." She lied. "Don't worry, Casey. We'll get out of here. Then we'll go home and we won't have to think about this ever again."

She closed her dark eyes and the boy heard a question echo in her brain.

Does home still exist?

Home had always been a nightmare for Casey, a hell where his mother could unleash her wrath upon him without fear of judging eyes. From inside the spiderweb of rope, Lucy's mind called out to his. The blond Mephistopheles dangled an escape from Perdition before his damaged psyche like a carrot. Through her, Efeu's talons tugged at him.

Home, he thought. The grip of Thule became an iron vice. In a fever dream, he saw the web encroaching around him. The mark of the Black Sun was a tarantula spinning cords of barbed wire. The fence that had once protected him became his prison. But the vision faded as swiftly as it had begun. Lucy's brainwaves gave way to the sound of approaching footsteps. Kikka's shadow filled the chamber's entrance. In her hand, she held an imitation Luger.

"Kikka." Lucy said. "What are you doing?"

Her sister did not answer. She walked as if in a daze, her eyes eerily vacant, eyes which fixed themselves on Casey.

"Why is it you?" She said. "We are supposed to be the special ones, not you. I have waited all my life for a promise to come true. Why is you and not me?"

"Stop this now!" Lucy snapped angrily. "This is treason."

"Shut up!" Her sister screamed. "Efeu wants to take my dream away? Fine!"

She pointed the Luger at Casey's face.

"Then I will take hers away too."

In the deciding instant that the trigger was pulled, Mrs Morgan leaped between her son and the fatal bullet. Casey heard the shot. He felt it too. The noise was so loud that it seemed as though someone had beat against his chest. He found himself shocked out of numbness by the sight of his mother's brains painting the floor. His feelings were mixed though. Should he still feel angry at her after such a deed? Did one final decent act warrant forgiveness for a lifetime of abuse? It was ironic, even in something as noble and selfless as sacrificing her own life, she had still succeeded in taking something from him and making it all about herself.

But Kikka's bloodlust was not yet sated. She pointed her pistol between the boy's eyes. Her hand shook, throwing her aim off. She was terrified, yet exhilarated at the same time. Casey stared Kikka down. He wore the same expression as his grandmother.

Disapproving.

Ashamed.

"Stop looking at me like that!" She screamed. Casey felt disgusted to be in this woman's presence. Her thoughts pushed against his brain. They reminded him of his mother and all her violence, of Kitty and her self-serving facade of friendship and of Sarah Lin's venomous words. There was no differentiating them anymore. They were all the same person, a shadowy spirit living in Kikka's body.

A black dragon.

The Untergeist.

Now, it would be their turn to know how he felt. In the spot where Kikka's pistol was pointed, a third eye opened. An eye as blue as the clear summer sky reflected in the ocean. His Mephistopheles laughed as the mark of the Black Sun began to glow. The castle's advanced technology obeyed his mental commands, creating a rupture in time and space. He thought that the phenomena resembled a black hole. Terror gripped Kikka as she was sucked into the vortex. He saw her frightened eyes, but felt nothing. He was a guard ushering her into the showers. Since she wanted to be an overman so badly, he treated her to their own Gehenna.

The Obsidian Realm.

Casey closed his third eye and the vortex disappeared. Just as Siegfried was made invincible by bathing in Fafnir's blood, the boy felt himself elevated beyond the constraints of mortal laws, to a place where the rules of good and evil do not apply.

Unchained from morality.

Unleashed amongst the sheep.

I am Casey, he thought. *I am KZ.*

The scent of almonds reached his nostrils, followed by a familiar voice calling to him from the darkness.

Share our glory, it whispered in his brain. *Share our glory.*

Efeu stood in the doorway. The boy had not even heard her approach. Cowering behind her was the wreck that had once been called Kitty. The dye had faded from her hair, just as the rebellion had faded from her spirit. She seemed like a pitiable creature now, following her new mistress's every step like a loyal hound. However, Casey's attention was pulled away from the girl by the force of his grandmother's superhuman will. The *fraulein* had changed into the military dress of her own nation, but was no less elegant for it. Indeed, it only seemed to enhance her exotic nature. She cut Lucy's bonds with a slash of her claws, freeing the blond Mephistopheles from the web of rope. She approached the edge of his fence and called to him with her mind.

Join our tribe.

Fight our war.

Share our glory.

"Are you really from Atlantis?" Casey asked. Efeu nodded.

"Unoa ekan habhjanan brenanan iuwiz ainaz schenkl." She replied in Runespeak.

"She says that she has brought you a birthday present from her Fatherland." Kitty translated. Casey raised a skeptical eyebrow.

"What kind of present?" He said.

"Ainaz ranken." The *fraulein* answered. *"Casey Morgan, Fuhrer von Uberwelt."*

"A title." Kitty explained. "Casey Morgan, Dictator of the Surface World."

"Habhjanan ainaz nett klingen, ne?"

"Has a nice ring to it, doesn't it?"

"It does." The boy replied. "I'm not sure if I'm up to the job, though."

"Wuryjanan ne."

"Do not worry."

"Ekan weljon wes nah furra min ling enkel."

"She will always be nearby to help her favourite grandson."

For the first time since he was a child, Casey felt like he could drop his fence for someone. The ropes fell to the ground, removing all obstacles between the *fraulein* and his heart. At last, he was hers. Casey ran over and hugged his grandmother. She embraced him in return, nursing him in her own brand of affection.

"Kwemanan." She said. *"Wiz motanan yai haim so iuwiz kunthyz schulen."*

"She wants you to go home with her so that you can train." Kitty translated.

"Hwa iuwiz rukkehr, iuwiz skul wes kuninaz von welt."

"When you return, you shall be master of the world."

Efeu raked her talons through Casey's long, copper locks with a frown.

"Wiz skul habhjanan zu tun etwas um dass wilthijaz haare."

"You will have to do something about that wild hair, though."

"Viele kande. Viele, viele."

"Many changes are in store. Many, many changes."

"I think I could use a little change." Casey said. "But what about Kitty? Is she coming with us?"

Efeu's expression grew stern.

"Da ischt ainaz stowijanan furra ihr in Thule ne. Auch wenn gab es, zi wurde sehwanan nur ubhilaz."

At the sound of her mistress's voice, Kitty's eyes turned downward in shame. Lucy gave her a cocky smile.

"There is no place for her in Atlantis." The blond woman explained. "Even if there were, she would see only monsters."

"Kwemanan no, ischt tiois furra os abreise."

"It is time for you to go now."

Efeu's third eye opened and her psionic powers radiated out like light from the sun. Her thoughts echoed into the cosmos, calling to something beyond the boundaries of the known world. To something even stronger than her. The message she sent was not mute to Casey's mind. He heard her broadcast it as clearly as a spoken word.

Requesting transport for two, General Vrilla.

From out of the endless darkness, from out of the bottomless sea, a voice replied to her telepathic call.

Request granted. Standby.

The black sun on the floor began to glow a bright blue. The light was so radiant that it was blinding. From within it, Casey heard the sounds of the ocean, of waves washing over the dry land.

Of his little sister laughing.

"Come on, Casey." He heard her say. "We've been waiting for you."

Could it really be her? Casey stepped towards the light, towards his lost family.

"Hurry up, slowpoke." Megan's voice teased, just like a little sister would. It felt wonderful to know that he was wanted.

The light is good, he thought. *Go towards the light.*

"Do not go!" Kitty yelled suddenly. "Please, Casey, stay here."

The future ruler of the world sighed.

"If you were offered a place in your Heaven, would you stay behind just because I begged you?" He asked. Kitty had no answer for him.

"Then you see why I have to go."

"No, Casey." The girl pleaded. "You have a gift. You were meant for great things."

"I know." He replied. "And I shall never achieve them while standing in your shadow."

The boy took another step.

Go towards the light.

"Casey, wait!" The girl cried.

Share our glory.

"Casey, stop!"

Share our glory.

***

Kitty watched as the two Atlanteans disappeared into the light, like moths consumed by an open flame. She knew that, despite his grandmother's promises, Casey would never return. Something would, of that she was certain. It would have his face, it would have his voice, but it would not have his soul. The boy that she had known and possibly could have spared from this fate was gone forever. The Black Sun's glow faded, then vanished completely, leaving only that crooked symbol on the ground as a sign that it had ever been there at all.

The blond Mephistopheles gave a victorious laugh. With her voice echoing through the castle, Lucy left the chamber to find her place in the new Reich of Darkness.

Listening to that laugh, Kitty felt completely and utterly alone.

Outside, the world she knew collapsed. It was Rome burning bright enough to light up the heavens. It was Babylon crushed beneath the weight of its own excesses. It was Atlantis sinking into the sea.

One kingdom fell, another rose.

There was no moral to the story, there was only history.

The End

"There is no true rebellion. Any movement, no matter how revolutionary it may seem, is nothing more than just another demographic."
-Translated from Efeu's private journals

Otto awoke to the sound of someone pounding violently on his front door. He rubbed his eyes wearily and made his way down the creaking steps to the entrance of his *hofbrau*.

It's probably just some drunk, he told himself. Although a much darker thought occurred to him as his eyes fell upon the portrait of Hitler that hung behind the bar, he shook it from his head in an instant. He had nothing to fear. He had always been faithful to the Reich.

He unlocked the door and opened it. As soon as he did, a girl of sixteen collapsed into his arms. She was fair-haired and quite pretty despite the dirt which soiled her olive dress.

In her side was a knife wound.

Otto glanced outside, but saw not a soul. So, he shut the door and dragged the unconscious young maiden into the kitchen where she would be out of sight. Once there, he propped her up in the nearest chair and believed that the situation called for a glass of whisky. He brought a cup full of the good stuff to her lips, hoping that the smell and aftertaste would snap her out of whatever dream state she was in. Although he was more than willing to sell it by the pint, Otto himself never cared much for alcohol. Slowly, he tipped the glass and watched the liquid disappear down the girl's gullet. Her eyes fluttered open, as if from a dream, and she coughed from her first taste of the spirits. She tried to rise, but collapsed back into the chair clutching her side in pain.

"Easy, *fraulein*," Otto said. He patted her shoulder.

"No," she replied, "you don't understand. I have to keep moving. I can't let him find me."

She tried to stand again, but fell straight onto the hard wood floor. She gritted her teeth from the wound in her ribs.

"How did you get that?" Otto asked, "who is chasing you?"

The girl studied him for a moment. Her eyes fell on her hand as she removed it from her side. It was covered in blood.

"If I give something to you, can you make sure it reaches the underground?" She asked. Otto was taken aback. Never before had he actually met anyone in the resistance. The fact that this girl could be one of them shocked him.

"Please," she said, "he'll find me soon. When he does, he'll kill me. There were six of us before. Me, Thea, Gottfried, Gustav, Erik and Anne. But he slaughtered all the rest."

"You say 'he'," Otto said, "a Gestapo officer?"

"Yes and no," the girl replied, "he said he was Gestapo. But he doesn't take his orders from Himmler. No, he let it slip that he works for someone called Efeu. I've heard of her in the underground. They say she's a sorceress."

"Now you're talking folklore," Otto said. But the girl shook her head.

"You have to believe me," she said, "this man, this... *thing*, he's inhuman. I watched him rip Anne's skull apart with his bare hands. Gustav, he gutted Gustav with an SS dagger. He then used that same dagger to slit Gottfried's throat."

"That is no proof that he's supernatural," Otto replied, "any man could do that if he were strong enough."

"No," the girl continued, "I emptied a Luger into him. I shot him in the heart. I shot him in the head. But he just kept coming. Then,... Erik and Thea,... he impaled them together on a flagpole. I'm the only one left now. Please, I have something important to give you."

She fished into her brassier and retrieved a small roll of film.

"Make sure this reaches the underground."

Before Otto could take the precious cargo from her hand, another knock came from the front door.

"Open up," said an unholy voice, "Gestapo."

Otto studied the girl. She seemed so pitiful.

So alone.

But his duties came first.

"The door is open," he called. Otto heard the entrance creak open, then slam shut. A pair of lead-booted footsteps approached. At the sound of each one, the terror in the girl's face grew.

Finally, a shrivelled figure in a Gestapo uniform stepped into the room. His face was bluish and shrunken, his eyes hidden behind reflective aviator glasses. Otto noted a number of bullet holes in his tunic. The figure grinned at the girl and drew a dagger from his belt.

"Thank you, sir," the creature wheezed, "you have done your Fuhrer a great service."

Otto turned away as the girl screamed. Her voice soon turned to gurgling as steel found skin.

Otto had nothing to fear. He had always been faithful to the Reich.

The End

CAPTAIN BLITZ

Part I

This Machine Kills Fascists

"I was not born with red eyes. They are an acquired feature. When I came of age in my homeland, I was stripped naked and thrown into a pit of dire reptiles. My superiors told me that, if I survived, I would be made immortal. Minutes later, I was the only living thing in that pit. I survived with nothing but my talons and talents to defend myself. But that was not the end of my evolution. When I joined The Wyrd Order, I was made to defy my newfound immortality and face death once more. How it happened is unimportant. Once I died, I descended into Helheim, where I saw what the surface dwellers would call the 'Norse Gods' in chains. My mission was simple; rescue one of those pagan idols from Hela's captivity. Armed once again with only my talons, I fought against an army of demons. But I succeeded in rescuing one deity in particular... Odin, the one-eyed king. To thank me, he gave me the power of his ocean blue eye. When I returned to the world of the living, my own eyes had turned red. A sign of accomplishment. A sign of distinction. Tell me now, in comparison, what makes you so noble?"

-Translated from Efeu's private journals

Chapter 1

Somewhere in the mists of the multiverse lies an ocean made of garbage. It is known as Sargasso, the trash heap of all existence. Its actual mechanics remain unknown, but it is believed that all lost or disposed-of things find their way there eventually. Nobody is sure how Captain Blitz's cryo-coffin ended up among the waters of sludge, but we can be assured that it did indeed end up there.

Uber Alice, that nasty Nazi who has sought to destroy democracy since the second world war, was rotting. Sargasso was a poison to her. Every minute that she spent there brought her one step closer to death. But, after what seemed like ages of sifting through the dirty dimension's mountains of refuse, she finally found her prize.

The cryo-coffin was cold to the touch. However, she knew how to change that. She entered the security code on the its control panel, stepped back and watched it open.

In his heyday, Captain Blitz had been a perfect specimen of a man. Large, muscular and unstoppable. But not even he was immune to Sargasso's rot. Half of the rubber skin on his face had deteriorated away, exposing a mess of rusting circuitry underneath. However, when he rose, he betrayed no weakness.

"Where am I?" He asked.

"Sargasso," Uber Alice replied, "you've been frozen since World War Two. Now that you're awake, we can use your powers to escape this blasted dimension and finally conquer the Earth!"

Captain Blitz saw the rot in Alice's skin and, in his robotic eyes, it penetrated all the way into her soul. He grabbed her by the throat and lifted her into the air.

"On the contrary," he said, "my mission is to eradicate degeneracy. I shall start with you!"

Chapter 2

Elsewhere in the multiverse lies the somewhat more famous kingdom of Atlantis. I'm sure it needs no introduction. Know only that it is a highly advanced aquatic civilization that connects to every ocean in existence.

Within the Temple of the Wyrd Order, two hooded figures walked calmly through hallways of gold and coral.

"We have a new mission for you, Lieutenant," said the shorter of the two, "do you remember your little social experiment on Earth from about a hundred years ago?"

"The Thule Society," the lieutenant replied.

"Yes," her superior answered, "you convinced them that they were descended from

Atlanteans."

"I'd hoped that they would establish a government that could work our interests in that dimension. It almost worked."

"Regardless," the superior officer continued, "one of their projects is now running loose on Kern."

She pressed her fingers next to her temple and, after great concentration, a blue eye opened on her forehead. Light poured forth from it, generating a hologram of Captain Blitz.

"We don't know for sure, but we think he ended up on Sargasso after the last mortal war. We do know that he has spent the last four days hopping dimensions. It's only a matter of time before he ends up here."

"General Vrilla," the lieutenant said, "with all due respect, I think the Kernians can handle one rogue android."

Vrilla grinned.

"My orders directly from Queen Nordica," she said, "and I quote, 'this is Efeu's mess, let her clean it up'."

Chapter 3

And so, events were set in motion. On the planet Kern, all trembled at the name of Captain Blitz.

All except one.

The android could not believe his eyes as he smashed through the building wall. He was so shocked by the figure in front of him that he didn't even notice the skyscraper collapse behind him.

"Mother?" He said.

The woman with crimson eyes nodded.

"Son," she answered, "your mission is over. You can come home now. Home to Atlantis."

Captain Blitz shook his head.

"No, Mother," he said, "there is still so much degeneracy in the world. Drugs. Sexuality. Crime. I must eradicate it. It's... it's my programming."

Efeu lowered her voice.

"Listen to me," she said, "we don't have a choice. If you can't stop on your own, I'll have to stop you."

"So be it," Captain Blitz replied. Efeu's expression turned hard as she spread her claws. She lunged at her robotic son, but even her superhuman physique proved no match for the machine. He struck her once and she fell limply to the ground.

"I'm sorry, Mother."

Part II

This Fascist Kills Machines

"What is The Wyrd Order? We were the witches who taunted Macbeth, the serpents who prophesied to Cassandra and the heads of the Beast whom John saw crawl from the sea. Our red eyes mark us as Atlantean nobility, not by birth but by merit. The third eye does not belong to us. It belongs to our God. In order to open it, we must concentrate on seeing the cosmos as he sees it. Once we do, it is not we who act, but him through us."

-Translated from Efeu's private journals

Chapter 1

After defeating Efeu, Captain Blitz fled Kern. His next target? Earth!

Walking through the streets of Ottawa, he spoke to himself.

"Look at this city. It reeks of corruption and degeneracy. Still, even I need a break. Perhaps this ugly building will prove entertaining."

He sneered as he entered the Canadian War Museum.

Chapter 2

"Is she alive?"

Efeu didn't know who asked the question. She opened her red eyes slowly and saw three figures in gas masks standing over her.

"Dude," one of them said to the others, "I don't even know what she is."

"Who are you people?" The Mistress of Misery asked weakly. The three figures cast their gazes upon her and backed away.

"We're the Kuka Crew," the leader of the trio

said, "trash collectors of the multiverse. There's actually millions of us all over the place, collecting the garbage that ends up in Sargasso."

"Did you see a super-powered robot?" Another asked, "'cause you look like you got beaten by a super-powered robot."

Efeu closed her eyes again and thought. She didn't know these creatures or how they could speak her language. But maybe she could use them.

"Mother!" Shouted a familiar voice. Efeu's eyes snapped open again at the sound, which she and the Kuka Crew followed to the edge of the surrounding rubble.

There stood Captain Blitz.

"For years, I looked up to you," he said, "I sought to eradicate degeneracy for you. But now I've learned that you were the degenerate all along."

"This guy's spooky," said the leader of the Kuka Crew as he aimed his plasma ring and...

Zap!

Captain Blitz plowed through the bolt of energy as if it were nothing.

Zap!

Zap!

More blasts followed, slowing the metal monstrosity down. His rubber skin began to peel off. Soon he was just mess of iron and circuits.

"Mother,... help me!"

"Stop calling me that! Efeu snapped. She plunged her talons into Captain Blitz's chest and tore out his processor. She tossed the piece of scrap to the Kuka Crew and sneered bitterly.

"Take this junk back to Sargasso."

The End

"And I saw a beast coming up out of the sea, having seven heads and ten horns, and upon his horns ten diadems, and upon his heads names of blasphemy. And the beast, which I saw, was like to a leopard, and his feet were as the feet of a bear, and his mouth as the mouth of a lion. And the dragon gave him his own strength, and great power. And I saw one of his heads as if it were slain to death: and his death's wound was healed. And all the earth was in admiration after the beast. And they adored the dragon, which gave power to the beast: and they adored the beast, saying: Who is like the beast? And who shall be able to fight with him? And there was given to him a mouth speaking great things and blasphemies: and power was given to him to do two and forty months. And he opened his mouth unto blasphemies against God, to blaspheme his name, and his tabernacle, and them that dwell in heaven. And it was given unto him to make war with the saints, and to overcome them. And power was given him over every tribe, and people, and tongue, and nation. And all that dwell upon the earth adored him, whose names are not written in the book of life of the Lamb, which was slain from the beginning of the world. If any man have an ear, let him hear. He that shall lead into captivity, shall go into captivity: he that shall kill by the sword, must be killed by the sword. Here is the patience and faith of the saints."

-Revelation 13:1-10